WHEN THE HILL CAME DOWN

SUSAN WHITE

WHEN THE HILL CAME DOWN

SUSAN WHITE

ACORN PRESS
CHARLOTTETOWN
2020

ACORNPRESS

P.O. Box 22024
Charlottetown, Prince Edward Island
C1A 9J2
acornpresscanada.com

Printed in Canada
Edited by Penelope Jackson
Designed by Matt Reid

Library and Archives Canada Cataloguing in Publication

Title: When the hill came down / Susan White.
Names: White, Susan, 1956- author.
Identifiers: Canadiana (print) 20200203436 | Canadiana (ebook)
20200255746 | ISBN 9781773660516
(softcover) | ISBN 9781773660561 (HTML)
Classification: LCC PS8645.H5467 W54 2020 | DDC C813/.6—dc23

The publisher acknowledges the support of the
Government of Canada, the Canada Council for the Arts,
and the province of Prince Edward Island.

To my dad

PART ONE
1969–1975

Summer Raine Barkley, a strange girl with an even stranger name; just a summer kid seen occasionally at Redmore's store, the wharf, or at an occasional community summer event, always feeling like she didn't belong. Just a summer kid, until June, when her parents sold their Fredericton home, deciding to live year-round in the Long Reach summer house. Long Reach, a long stretch of rough, hilly dirt road from the St. James Anglican Church to the Westfield ferry beside the meandering Saint John River.

Summer knew she didn't actually live in Long Reach. She understood the Barkley property was in Grey's Mills. Grey's Mills, The Cedars, Long Reach, Whites Bluff, Holderville, Bedford, Ghost Hollow, Carter's and Harding's Point; she knew the names but had only a vague idea of the boundaries. And confusion about place names and where they stopped and started was apparently proof positive that Summer Barkley was not from here.

The name "Barkley," however, had been part of the Long Reach vernacular for generations. Summer's father had actually been born in the very house neighbours now considered to be the Barkleys' summer place. Donald Barkley had attended the one-room schoolhouse, which was now the Evanses' summer place, with children who were now the parents of some of the kids his thirteen-year-old daughter, Summer, would be going to Macdonald Consolidated School with.

The original Barkleys who settled on the land and gave the stream of water at the bottom of the hill the name "Barkley's Brook" had received a land grant, as had the descendants of most of the other families inhabiting parcels of the land stretching from Barkley's Brook to the Westfield ferry. Hundreds arrived as United Empire Loyalists, having made the choice to remain loyal to the King and to England during the upheaval of the American Revolutionary War. The Barkley ancestors cleared and farmed the land beside the Saint John River, and the Barkley name had been on the Kingston Peninsula census for almost two hundred years.

Summer knew the Barkley family history and felt a deep connection to the place she'd been coming to every summer her entire life. But this morning as she walked alone up the driveway to wait for the school bus, knowledge that her descendants had walked this ground for generations gave her no comfort. It would be so much easier if Hudson was walking to the bus stop with her, but of course they'd still be in Fredericton if Hudson were here. He'd be walking up the hill to Montgomery Street School and she'd be walking to Albert Street Junior High with Doris and Wendy, anxious for her first day in grade seven.

Mr. Titus opened the bus door and greeted Summer. Maybe the butterflies would settle and she wouldn't throw up. She slid into the first empty seat without looking at the kids behind, feeling their stares as if she were an alien specimen brought back from the moon. Summer had seen Neil Armstrong walk on the moon in July on the small portable TV Dad had borrowed so they could watch the Apollo landing. Even after Dad stuck balled aluminum on the antenna, the picture remained fuzzy, making the monumental event barely visible but highlighting the moon's strange surface and uninhabitable atmosphere. Heading to a new school seemed just as frightening and perilous.

As Mr. Titus geared up and pulled onto the road, the noise level rose. Summer stared out the bus window, trying to settle her nerves and prepare for what was to come. Once across the Barkley Brook Bridge the dirt road changed to pavement. Apparently, the dirt stretch was going to be paved in the spring as one of the promises the Robichaud government was making to rural New Brunswick. A promise called Equal Opportunity had closed the last one-room schoolhouse two years ago, and now all school-age children on the peninsula rode yellow buses to the big school Summer was heading toward.

The pavement always seemed to Summer the separation between her beloved summer retreat and the journey home. Sometimes Dad drove home by way of Westfield and they wouldn't see pavement until they crossed the ferry and drove up the River Road toward Fredericton. But usually Dad chose the smoother trip toward Hampton and up through Cambridge Narrows, where they would hit dirt again for a short distance.

But this morning, watching the pavement unfurl, Summer knew her destination was not her familiar life in Fredericton, but the building at the top of Kingston hill she'd passed so many times, never imagining she'd be a student there someday. And what had she been thinking when choosing her outfit this morning? She'd feel quite confident about the style and acceptability of the striped Twiggy dress she'd chosen to wear if she was walking into Albert Street surrounded by her friends.

She'd be just a grade seven kid, not a new kid, at Albert Street School. Summer had lived in the Regent Street house all her life, gone to school with the same kids and had several good friends who lived in houses on nearby streets. People knew Summer Barkley, and she'd always felt like she belonged. But being Summer Barkley in Fredericton wasn't the same as it used to be, and she hated that change and the new labels it gave her: poor Summer Barkley, Hudson Barkley's sister, the sister of the boy who had died at the Lady Beaverbrook Rink. The Barkleys were now the family of the dead boy, and whispers of the shocking accident now followed her and her parents everywhere they went in their hometown.

Summer knew she would stick out as the new kid at this new school no matter what she was wearing, but she wouldn't get the looks of pity. She wouldn't hear the whispered comments when she walked into the room. If she was talked about today, the reasons would be totally different.

Summer pulled her journal out of the front pocket of her book bag. She removed the top from her fountain pen. This morning she'd attached the green ink cartridge, excited with her colour choice and the endless possibility of the words she might write with it. Trying to keep control with the swaying motion of the bus, she put pen to paper, preparing the page's heading in her distinctive cursive:

> Summer Barkley, September 4, 1969
> Grade seven, Macdonald Consolidated School
>
> I am on my way to my new school. I will get through my
> first day and make the best of whatever this day brings.
> I am Summer Raine Barkley and I belong here.

Summer didn't take any more notice of the bus ride until Mr. Titus pulled the bus up to the school and opened the door. She'd quickly capped her pen, closed her journal, and tucked it back into her book bag. Slinging the bag over her shoulder, she followed the others through the main door of the school, where her panic instantly returned. She had no idea which direction to go or where to find the grade seven classrooms.

Standing stupidly, looking the part of a new kid, probably was what caught the attention of a man standing at the office door, who Summer quickly concluded was the principal. Mr. McGuire introduced himself, said her name, grade, and homeroom teacher, and motioned for her to follow him down the hall, through a set of double doors, and up a steep set of stairs. Apparently not many new students were arriving today.

"Throw him out, boys. Getting thrown down a few steps isn't going to hurt him. Dropping two storeys jumbled his brain, and you can't fix stupid."

Summer Barkley heard laughter coming from an opening off a landing at the top of the first section of the stairway. She kept walking until she could see that a doorway to the left of the landing had several steps leading to what she quickly deduced was a boys' washroom. A boy tumbled down the few steps, hitting the landing floor inches from her feet.

The laughter continued and seemed far from friendly and playful. Summer took in the expression on the face of the tall, gangly boy sprawled out on the hardwood landing.

Mr. McGuire thundered up into the washroom, two steps at a time.

"Get out. Is this really how you boys want to start this school year? You all know better than to hang out with Winston. Winston Rideout, I'm not putting up with any of your foolishness. I don't have to keep you after you turn eighteen, and if I remember correctly you have a birthday real soon. Do you think you could smarten up and at least get yourself out of grade seven before we kick you out? And don't think I can't smell the smoke in here, boys."

Four boys sheepishly exited the washroom. Mr. McGuire held tightly to the collar of a fifth boy's shirt as he escorted him down the four stairs. Summer assumed this was Winston Rideout, and he no longer looked like the tough guy she'd heard seconds earlier telling his friends to throw someone down the stairs in a heap.

Mr. McGuire extended his hand to the boy on the floor. "Get up, Keefe. You know better than to go in the washroom before the second bell. You're at the mercy of those hooligans when there's no teacher upstairs."

Not wanting to embarrass the boy, who looked toward her as he got to his feet, Summer quickly turned and walked up the remaining stairs. The big guy Mr. McGuire had just pulled from the washroom was in grade *seven*. Summer hoped there was more than one class of grade sevens, because she didn't want him in her class. How could he have called the other guy stupid when he was almost eighteen and in grade seven? Last year her grade six class at Montgomery St. had one boy who was one year older than the rest, but what kind of a school was this, with kids in a class who were five years older than they should be? Summer wondered what grade the guy being called stupid was in.

Mr. McGuire herded the group of boys into their classroom and said, "Now, perhaps you young men could show some manners and not scare the life out of this new young lady. This is your classroom, Miss Barkley. Let me assure you, not all your classmates are as badly behaved. Keefe, come with me and I'll get you to help Mr. Wheaton get the chairs set up for the assembly."

The tall boy turned and followed the principal just as a woman topped the stairs and gave a loud command for everyone to get in the classroom, take a seat, and settle down.

"How come the retards get to put chairs out and we have to do work?" Winston Rideout asked in a loud voice.

"Winston. Sit down and be quiet. You'll do what you're told or head right down to Mr. McGuire's office. Don't even bother unpacking your book bag if you don't plan on doing any work. Why do you think you're in my class? Mr. McGuire wouldn't give you to a brand-new teacher. Poor Miss Dunphy would quit before the day was over if she had to put up with the likes of you."

"Miss Dumb-phy. That's a good name for a teacher for those dummies. Now I'm happy I'm in your class, Mrs. Thompson. And I'm glad Keefe Williams ain't in our class. Stupid rubs off, you know."

"I said sit down and be quiet," Mrs. Thompson said sternly. "Now listen for your names as I call the roll."

Summer looked around at the other students crowded into the classroom as Mrs. Thompson called out the names on her list. A girl named Debbie actually smiled when Summer looked over her way. And a girl named Valerie sitting in the desk beside Summer nodded and said hi.

Summer's nervousness returned as she filed down the stairs with the crowd at recess time. She would rather have stayed in the classroom, happy to have Mrs. Thompson, who had not stopped talking since the morning started, protect her from having to mingle with these kids who were all strangers to her. Heading out to the playground, she might have to speak to someone.

"What kind of a name is Summer?" Winston Rideout called out as he came up behind her on the stairs. "Do you change it when summer's over? Will we call you Fall and then Winter and Spring?" He let out a loud laugh and pushed into her, almost causing her to stumble on the last step.

"Don't be a jerk, Winston. Leave her alone," Debbie said.

*

Keefe Williams leaned against the tree at the far end of the empty schoolyard. Mr. Wheaton had let him leave a few minutes before the bell. He'd carried stacks of ten wooden chairs at once, and it hadn't taken him long to set the rows up for the assembly. "All brawn, no brains," Uncle Tom always said.

Shortly after the bell rang the doors opened and the throng of kids poured out. Keefe found himself looking at the bodies streaming through the doors, trying to see the girl who'd stared down at him earlier. The look he'd seen on her face was not a familiar one. It wasn't pity or disinterest and it wasn't disgust. He wasn't sure what it was, but it hadn't left him feeling the way he usually felt. She was new. Maybe there was one person in this school, on this whole crappy peninsula, who might really see him for once. She had no idea who he was and maybe it could stay that way for at least a day or two.

Summer followed Debbie out the door and joined a group of girls standing by the fence separating the parking lot from the playground. She recognized a girl she'd met at the wharf last week. The girl was smiling and looked toward her as if she might be going to give her a friendly greeting. Maybe she could get through recess after all.

"I love your bell bottoms, Deb. Where did you get them?"

The smile and enthusiastic reception was not a "Welcome to our school" greeting after all, but a fashion assessment instead, and it had not been directed at her. Summer took her place in the circle of chatty, excited girls and looked out over Debbie's head, wishing she were standing with the familiar group of friends she'd known since first grade, who were probably gathering outside Albert Street School in Fredericton right now. Grade seven was definitely not the best grade to start making new friends.

Summer could see the boy from the landing standing alone on the playground, and he seemed to be looking her way. She could see Winston's crowd a few feet away from him, but Mr. McGuire was standing nearby. Winston probably wouldn't go after the boy within arm's reach of Mr. McGuire.

A few minutes later the bell rang, and as she and Debbie walked back into the school, Summer asked about the boy she'd watched for the entire recess.

"His name is Keefe. Keefe Williams. Isn't that the meanest

thing ever? Why didn't his parents call him some normal name, or at least call him Keith? 'Keefe' just sounds like you're not saying his name right."

Summer didn't say anything. She'd heard her fair share of opinions about her name for as long as she could remember. She had come home crying her first day of grade one because the teacher said "Summer" was a stupid name and she would call her by her middle name. When Summer told Mrs. Clark her middle name was Raine, she said she was going to call her Jane, which rhymed with rain but was a good, sensible, civilized name.

An immediate visit to the school by Summer's parents resulted in a change of teachers, since apparently, nothing they or the principal said could change Mrs. Clark's attitude, and she refused to call a little girl in her class by the name of a season. A change of teacher had been the best solution, as they felt Mrs. Clarke's name opinions might not be her only unwavering viewpoint. Mrs. MacGregor had been the nicest teacher anyone could want and had not skipped a beat when Summer entered her classroom the next day and stated her full name. Mrs. Macgregor said the name was just as lovely as the little girl who bore the name appeared to be.

Keefe. Summer didn't think there was a thing wrong with the name, and she also thought he was kind of cute, but she certainly wasn't going to offer her opinion to Debbie, who was continuing to share some other details about Keefe Williams.

"He's failed a lot. My sister was in his class in grade three and he was with my brother in grade five. He was in grade six with me last year. The teacher hollered at him all the time. He got mad one day and knocked his desk over and got kicked out. I think he stayed home most of May and June. I say 'home,' but he doesn't really have a home. He lives all over the place. He goes on my bus when he stays at the Fullertons'. He'll probably be back there pretty soon, because Raymond Fullerton has fields of turnips to harvest and potatoes to dig."

Summer was hanging her sweater in the coatroom when she saw Keefe heading toward the grade seven classroom across the hall. He turned his head slightly and nodded at her. His smile had calmness and his eyes a certain warmth, giving him an expression very different from the troubled one she had seen on his face as he lay sprawled on the landing earlier. Summer nodded back at Keefe Williams and walked into her classroom.

*

Don Barkley got right to work on the woodpile after watching from the upstairs window, making sure Summer got on the bus. He'd wanted to walk up with her but knew his grade-seven daughter did not need her daddy waiting at the bus stop with her on her first day at a new school. He would put three ranks in the basement and then pile the rest of the seven cords of hardwood Bill Titus delivered yesterday into the woodshed. He had no idea how much wood they would need to get them through the winter. This was just one of his worries.

Summer had tried so hard to mask her nervousness this morning. It was a hard age to arrive at a new school in a community she'd only known in the summer. Was he being selfish bringing her here? And how thrilled was Marilyn to be here year-round? Was he just escaping things by moving his family to the peninsula?

Don threw the stick of hardwood into the wheelbarrow, trying to keep his emotions at bay. His family. Being asked how many children he had was one of the hardest questions to face. His family now only included his daughter and his wife, but he could not leave his son out when he answered that casual question. There was nothing casual about it for him. Telling perfect strangers about Hudson was one of the main reasons for the move. In Fredericton, his answer was always met with the look and the same response: "Oh, that was *your* boy."

But moving had not made answering the question any easier. Now it was friends from childhood and summer acquaintances he had to tell of his son's death. The telling varied from the quick statement, "We lost our son eight months ago," to a more detailed explanation. It never got easier, even though he sometimes heard himself reciting the details as if it were someone else's story. As if the horror of that moment had somehow evaporated. It sounded farfetched to him even as he repeated it. Ten-year-old boys do not die simply by falling on the ice.

Don wheeled the wheelbarrow to the cellar opening. He

could still see it in his mind, replayed in slow motion just as it had that night. Hudson had been standing with a group of friends near the penalty box. The Fredericton High School games always caused excitement among the younger crowd, but the provincial championship had been intense. In the final seconds, Fredericton had tied the game and the game had gone to sudden death.

Sudden death. Those words reverberated in the very core of his being. From six rows back he'd watched his son along with the boys beside him tumble over the boards to join the celebration on the ice. Tumbling over in a mass of young bodies. He had stood with the crowd, cheering, and hadn't seen the commotion at first as the coach, several parents, and Dr. Taylor, who always stood by ready to check out injured players, had rushed on to the ice.

He heard the buzz through the stands. A boy was not getting up. Somebody was hurt on the ice. He heard a woman say, "Toronto Maple Leaf jersey." He got to Hudson at the same time the ambulance attendants did. He looked asleep. Sudden death.

My son died from a fall on the ice. It never seemed believable when he said it. It had never seemed believable. As he watched them put Hudson on the stretcher and carry him from the rink he cried out that this could not be true. His son had just moments earlier been alive, healthy, just a regular boy caught up in the excitement of his beloved sport. He had proudly worn his jersey with Sawchuk's number emblazoned on the back to the game, as a good-luck charm for the home team.

When Marilyn met him at the Victoria General emergency room, he had to tell her that their son was dead. Now, months later, the reality of that freak accident was no easier to talk about and certainly no easier to live with.

*

It was the third week of school before Summer was told the fact most commonly referred to whenever anyone talked about Keefe Williams. In those weeks, the first nods she and Keefe had given each other had been followed by many more, and it seemed several times a day Summer would spot the boy who had caught her interest on her first morning at MCS.

Summer didn't have the same lost, frightened feeling she'd had the first morning. She had made several friends, including a girl named Nancy. She'd met most kids in both grade-seven classes, but despite the nods she and Keefe exchanged, they had not said one word to each other. Her new friends said similar things to what Debbie had told her about Keefe Williams, referring to his poor grades, his trouble at school, and his lack of a home. But on the third week when Keefe boarded Summer's bus after school, Nancy whispered another fact as he walked by.

"His parents died. He got thrown out the window when—"

Billy Shamper pulled Nancy's ponytail, leaving the rest of her whispered revelation untold. Summer turned slightly, not wanting to be too obvious, and watched Keefe take his seat across the aisle, two rows back. He hoisted his duffle bag onto the seat beside him.

"Where you going now, Freddy Freeloader?" a kid at the back hollered out.

Keefe didn't respond but stared out the bus window.

"He lives with his uncle and doesn't usually take our bus, but he's going to Smith's," Nancy said, apparently forgetting she had left out the details of why Keefe Williams had been thrown out a window. "Mr. Smith always has hardwood to split and deliver this time of year. Teddy says Keefe is going there for a couple of weeks. They'll keep him out of school until the wood gets done."

Summer remembered Winston Rideout saying something about a two-storey fall before he threw Keefe from the boys' washroom on the first day of school. Summer wondered what had happened to his parents. A fire, maybe. Maybe his parents had died in a fire but had thrown him out an upstairs window to save his life. How mean of everyone to talk about it like it was Keefe's fault something so terrible had happened to him when he was just a baby. Why was everyone so mean to him, and if he lived with his uncle, why did he get passed around from place to place, working like an adult?

Summer took a book from her bag. She opened the hardcover volume of *Anne of Avonlea*, hoping it might give Nancy the message she didn't want to talk. If Keefe was out of school for a while, she wouldn't get to see him. As Summer stared at the page, pretending to read, she realized how much she had looked forward to catching a glimpse of Keefe Williams every day since starting at her new school three weeks ago.

*

Every night after supper Summer rode her bike to the bridge. Climbing down the bank and sitting beside the wide brook, writing her thoughts into her leather bound journal, made evenings more bearable. It was so hard watching her parents. Despite them trying to put on a good front, she knew Hudson's upcoming birthday was heavy on their minds.

It was beginning to get dark, but Summer was reluctant to get up and head back home. She turned the next page. Her bike had a reflector on the front and back and the ride home was a short one. She was intently writing the words to best describe the sun dipping below the hill when a noise from behind startled her and she jumped to her feet.

"Sorry, I didn't mean to scare you."

Keefe Williams was standing just a few feet away from her.

"I didn't hear you walk down the bank."

"I can see why. You were busy."

"My name is Summer, Summer Barkley. I come here every night. My driveway is just up the hill."

"I know your name and I know where you live."

"You do?"

"I saw you get off the bus yesterday. And of course I know your name. We don't get many new kids. And all the boys get real excited when the new kid is a girl, so it doesn't take long for her name to get told around. I knew your name the first morning. It always helps to know the name of the girl who just saw you get made a fool of."

"I didn't think you were a fool. It wasn't your fault. It wouldn't take even a new girl long to figure out Winston Rideout's the fool, not you. I'm sorry I stared at you, though."

"I'm used to it. It's getting dark. You better be getting home. I don't usually get to stop work until after dark but there was prayer meeting tonight and Mr. Smith knocked off early. Prayer meeting. You'd be surprised what I know about those good men who go off to prayer meeting every Wednesday night."

"They say you won't be at school for a couple of weeks."

"I can only imagine what else they say. No, I'll be at the Smiths' for a couple of weeks and then I expect old man Fullerton will be ready for me. Then it will be my Uncle Tom's turn. I'll be lucky if I get back to school before March."

"What do you mean? It's the law. You've got to stay in school till you're at least sixteen, don't you? You're not older than sixteen, are you?"

"No, despite how stupid I'm sure they've told you I am, I'm only fifteen. Just turned fifteen in April. But the way things work around here is, the truant officer overlooks my lack of attendance, trusting my guardianship to my uncle, probably so the province doesn't have to pay for my room and board. It's a long story, but you better hop on your bike and get on home. I'm sure your parents wouldn't want you hanging out here with the likes of me after dark."

"What do mean, 'the likes of you?' Besides, my parents don't judge people. They make up their minds about folks by what they see, same as I do, and not by what other people tell them. Nothing I've seen yet makes me think I'm in any danger being here with you, dark or daylight."

"Well thanks, I guess. Maybe I'll run into you again."

"I come here every night. I like it here. The brook helps me think. It's the running water, I guess."

"Well, if you like running water, maybe you would like to go for a walk in the wood road across the way sometime. There's a nice waterfall back there. Real peaceful place, I think."

"Does Mr. Smith give you any time off during the daylight?"

"He doesn't make me work at the wood on Sunday, being a good Christian and all. Mind you, he makes sure I do the milking for him and any other chores that need doing. But last year he gave me Sunday afternoons off. I made sure I hightailed it off his place on Sunday afternoons so he wouldn't change his mind and find work for me to do. I was wandering around on the Henderson place when I found the waterfall."

"Well, if I don't see you before then, let's meet here on Sunday afternoon and we can walk in to see the waterfall. Maybe I could get my mom to make us up a picnic or something."

"I certainly wouldn't say no to a picnic. I do get enough to eat at the Smiths' though. Mrs. Smith isn't a bad cook, and the Smiths sure aren't the stingiest place around when it comes to feeding me.

Summer and Keefe climbed the bank and stepped over the guardrail to where Summer's bike was propped up against the bridge.

"How about two o'clock on Sunday, then?" Summer asked.

"Sure thing," Keefe replied. "Two o'clock Sunday afternoon it is. See you then, Summer Barkley."

"See you then, Keefe Williams," Summer said as she hopped on her bike and rode off up the hill.

*

Summer resisted the temptation to mention her plans for Sunday to anyone. She was pretty sure Debbie would not understand why she would want to spend any time with Keefe Williams. Debbie was boy crazy. Every day at school Debbie seemed to be bonkers over a different boy. Her latest heart-throb was Winston Rideout. Summer hadn't said one word about her choice but was quite sure Debbie wouldn't offer her the same courtesy if she told Debbie she liked Keefe Williams and had plans to meet him at the brook on Sunday afternoon.

Friday after school she and Nancy biked by the Smiths' house and she saw Keefe in the yard, piling hardwood. Summer pretended to have a rock in her shoe and got off her bike at the Smiths' mailbox to remove the imaginary pebble. Keefe looked up but didn't acknowledge her at all. Maybe he wouldn't even show up, but either way she wasn't telling Debbie or Nancy how much she was looking forward to seeing him again.

On Sunday Summer told her mother where she was going

just a few minutes before asking her to pack a picnic lunch for her and the friend she was meeting at the bridge.

"What's your friend's name?" Marilyn Barkley asked, with a tone indicating she suspected this new friend might be a boy.

"Keefe Williams," Summer answered.

"Williams?" Don Barkley asked. "When I was a kid I used to pick raspberries for a Joe Cronk, and his daughter was married to a Williams. Is this boy his grandson, do you know?"

"I don't know," Summer answered. "His parents are dead."

"Really? The poor kid," Marilyn Barkley said. "Is he a nice boy? Should your father or I go on this picnic with you?"

"Oh, Mom," Summer said. "We're just going for a walk. He says there's a waterfall up Sanford Henderson's wood road. He's very nice."

"Very nice? Marilyn, our girl thinks this boy is *very* nice."

"Well, maybe you should bring him down to meet us after this walk of yours."

"Mom, I don't want to scare him off. I'm just getting to know him. I'll let you know after our afternoon together if I want to invite him to our house. He doesn't have a lot of free time, though."

"Why?" Don Barkley asked. "Does he have a job or something? How old is this boy?"

"He's only fifteen. He doesn't have a job really, but he does have to work. He goes to people's houses and works for them. I don't think they pay him. I think they just feed him and give him a place to stay."

"That's terrible. Seems like something you'd hear happening years ago, not this day and age. Why hasn't he been adopted or put into foster care or an orphanage?"

"He lives with his uncle, and that's who sends him to work for people, I think. I don't know, Mom. I've only talked to him once. I don't know his whole life history."

"Here. Let me put a few more cookies in the basket. Poor kid might not be getting enough to eat."

"He said the Smiths feed him good. He said some places don't, though. I can't imagine going from place to place and not having a real home and your own family. I feel sorry for him. The other kids don't treat him very nice."

"Leave it to our daughter to take in the underdog, Marilyn. She always did bring home the wounded birds and lost puppies."

"Oh, Dad. Keefe is not a puppy and he's not wounded. I'm not seeing him because I feel sorry for him. He's nice. Now I've got to get going. I don't want him to get to the bridge and think I'm not coming."

"Invite him for supper sometime. See when he can get away. Surely the Smiths aren't slave drivers and would let him visit the neighbours now and again."

"I'll ask him, Mom, if he even shows up. Maybe it's me in danger of getting stood up. He might have just been teasing the new girl."

*

22

As she topped the hill, Summer could see Keefe, his back toward her, leaning against the bridge. She'd walked instead of bringing her bike, worried the full basket would spill if she hung it from her handlebars or tried to balance it on her lap. Mom had stuffed enough food into the rectangular basket to feed ten people and folded up a grocery bag and stuck it in so Keefe could take the leftovers back with him.

As she started down the hill, Summer realized she looked like Little Red Riding Hood on her way to Grandmother's house. She should have brought the food in her backpack and not looked like such a dork.

Keefe turned toward her and ran up the hill to meet her. "Let me take the basket."

"It's heavy. My mother loves to feed people and took the packing of our picnic very seriously."

"Nice. The walk to the waterfall is quite long. We'll be ready for a snack by the time we get there."

"Oh, this is more than a snack."

The walk across the field was silent, but when they stepped on to the wood road trail Keefe started talking as if he had been rehearsing exactly what he was going to say. The words came out matter-of-factly and in a long, uninterrupted dialogue.

"My parents died when I was three weeks old. I have never even seen a picture of them. The house was destroyed and they were killed. Suffocated, they say, when the house collapsed and the mud came in. It sounds crazy, and I don't talk about it, but I want you to know what happened. People talk about it as if it was a horror movie. People tell the story like I was an extra or a prop. Just an afterthought in the good story it makes when a whole house fills with the rushing flood of an avalanche of mud, rocks, and debris, knocking out windows and collapsing walls. She threw me out. They don't know for sure it was her, but I like to think it was. I landed on the roof of the veranda and somehow I was still there when they found it on the ground hours later. 'Wrapped up in a blanket and not even crying,' my aunt Helen always said. That's what they base their theory of me being simple on. A baby wide-eyed and not even crying after dropping two storeys must have some damage to his brain. Plus, the fact I didn't talk until I was four years old.

"I wanted to tell you the story myself. The damn story seems to be all anyone cares to know about me. You would think after fifteen years it might fade, but instead it just gets better, more farfetched, and more entertaining, apparently, to everyone but me. I would be happy if I never heard the story again. I thought about not telling you and just enjoying knowing one person who doesn't know the story. But I figured you probably knew it by now anyway and wouldn't even show up."

"Why did you think I wouldn't show up if I knew it? I didn't hear it, by the way. The only thing I heard was your parents were dead and you had been thrown out the window."

"Oh yeah, that's their favourite part. I only get teased about it a few times a day at school. It doesn't come up much when

I'm somewhere working, although I have heard whispered references to it. And it's not only the kids; the teachers I've had like to bring it up one way or another to explain any trouble I have, whether doing long division or failing a test on the British monarchy. It's either in a nice, sappy, pitiful way, like 'The poor little boy took an awful blow to head,' or the not-so-nice ones. 'He's dumb as dirt' was a favourite of my grade six teachers.

"That's awful, Keefe."

"Oh, you get used to it. I'm not dumb, just so you know. There are lots of things I can do, just so happens reading and spelling aren't two of them. I can do math, though, despite getting a little fetched up on long division in grade four. It could have been the fact that Miss Harvey didn't know how to teach it. I'm not sure she even knew how to do it."

"I know what it's like to be known by a story. My brother died from an accident almost a year ago."

"I'm sorry."

"Thanks. My brother was ten. His name was Hudson. After he died people in Fredericton always called him 'the boy who fell on the ice and died.' It made me mad when they wouldn't even use his name. You don't need to mention your story to me ever again if you don't want to. I don't care what other people say about you. I want to get to know you, or I wouldn't have come. I was worried you would back out, you know."

"Why would I back out? The new girl asked me to have a picnic with her."

"Let's both talk about other things. For starters, tell me one of those things you do really well."

"I wasn't going to show you until we got to the falls, but since you asked." Keefe pulled a folded piece of paper out of his back pocket and passed it to Summer.

Summer unfolded the paper and what she saw made her stop walking. She sat on a nearby log to have a good look at a drawing of a landscape of trees and rocks framing a beautiful waterfall. Every detail was perfect, and even though the sketch was done with pencil, she could almost imagine colours in the lush scene.

"Is this the waterfall we're going to? Did you draw this?"

"Yeah."

"It is amazing."

"You can have it. It's just pencil and I did it in a hurry. I'm saving up my money to get some art supplies. It would be better if I could do it with pastels or paint, although I've never had either. It would look nicer in colour, I think."

"It is beautiful just the way it is. You should keep it. You should show someone. Mr. Hartt, maybe. Surely an art teacher could see how talented you are."

"No way. I'm not showing anyone. You can have it if you want. Maybe when I get more money saved you could buy the supplies for me. You probably get to Saint John more often than I do. The only time I go is when I go with a farmer to deliver vegetables or with Uncle Tom to take pulpwood to the mill."

"Is your uncle the only family you have?"

"I don't want to talk about it. Let's keep going so you can see the waterfall and see if I'm really as good at drawing as you think I am."

*

After their time together on Sunday, Summer and Keefe saw each other every night for the next week. After Keefe finished a day of work at the Smiths', he would walk up to the Barkleys'. The first night, Marilyn Barkley saved a plate of supper for him in case he was hungry.

"Mom, he is not here to eat. He already had his supper."

"It does look good, though, Mrs. Barkley. I wouldn't want it to go to waste."

Keefe sat at the kitchen table eating while Don Barkley sat across from him doing most of the talking. Summer and her mother stood at the sink doing up the supper dishes.

The next night Keefe arrived in time to eat supper with the family. After cleanup Summer and Keefe sat alone in the TV room and fell into the comfortable chatter that had come so easy by the end of their picnic. It already felt to Summer like she had known Keefe Williams for a long time.

"I didn't think this waterfall could be more beautiful," Keefe said as he passed Summer a folded piece of paper. "I finished what I started sketching at the falls on Sunday."

"I'm impressed you can draw people as good as you can draw trees and rocks. It looks just like me."

"Thanks."

"You need pastels, paints, sketchpads, canvas, an easel, and brushes. If this is what you can do with a pencil I can only imagine what you can do with real art supplies. How much money do you have saved?"

"I have almost fifteen dollars. I only get a few cents here and there, sometimes a dollar or two when I deliver wood with Mr. Smith. The people feel sorry for me, I guess."

"You work for no pay?"

"They pay Uncle Tom some after they cover my room and board. It's the deal, I guess. Tom rents me out."

"How long has he been doing that?"

"A long time. Right after my Aunt Helen died. I was always a good worker, and once he realized he could make a bit of money off me as well as not having to feed me, he saw an opportunity too good to pass up. He buys my clothes, but as you can see, not too often. These jeans are halfway up my legs, and if it wasn't for the patches they'd be no pants at all. 'Williams, you should have a party and invite the bottom of your pants' or 'We expecting a flood?' Yeah, nothing better than wearing pants two sizes too small to make sure you stick out worse than you already do."

"He gets money for you and he doesn't even buy you the stuff you need. That's terrible."

"It could be worse. I could live with him all the time. He

gets me to work for him now and again, and believe me, two or three weeks at a time with him is plenty. But enough about me."

*

"I'm only at the Smiths' for one more week," Keefe said on Saturday evening. "I'll be going to Fullerton's after this, and it's too far to walk up to visit. I don't know if I'll be able to get up on the weekend, even if he gives me any time off."

"You probably don't have a bike, do you?"

"No, I don't. I don't even know how to ride one. Pretty bad, eh? But I've never had one to learn on, and by the time you get to be my age it's pretty embarrassing to let anyone see you try. Training wheels would look real dumb."

"Dad has a bike. Why don't you try to ride it? So what if you fall a couple of times? Nobody here is going to make fun of you. You can ride it around here every day until you get used to it. I am sure Dad would let you take it to Fullerton's. Then you could bike up when you have some time off."

"Really. He wouldn't mind?"

"No, I'm sure he wouldn't. He doesn't use it anymore. Come on, let's go outside and you can try it. You're allowed to fall six times, and then I might have to laugh at you."

*

The late-October air had a bite to it, and Summer stopped her bike at the top of MacDougall's hill to zip up her jacket.

Keefe was biking to Redmore's store to meet her after a long day of pulling turnips. Yesterday would have been Hudson's eleventh birthday. It had been a rough week for them all, especially Dad. On Wednesday after school she had found him sitting on the floor in Hudson's room crying. She'd walked by without going in.

Nothing had been changed in Hudson's bedroom. All his summer treasures were still on display. They had of course cleaned out his bedroom in Fredericton when they moved, and Mom had stuck the box of the items she'd saved in the closet of his room here. Hudson would have loved living here year-round. He would have loved watching the leaves turn colour on the trees. He would have watched the river daily, anxiously waiting for it to freeze. Hudson loved skating and would have loved to be able to just walk to the river to skate. He'd spent just about every day at the Lady Beaverbrook Rink once the ice was in.

Summer could see her dad's green bike propped up against the payphone when she topped Carvell's hill. Most nights since Keefe went to Fullerton's he had managed to get to the payphone at Redmore's to call her. It was during last night's call they'd made the plan to meet here and then bike back to Summer's house for supper. Dad would drive Keefe back down to Fullerton's later.

Summer set her bike on the ground and headed toward the store as Keefe came out the door with two bottles of Coca-Cola.

"This is our first real date," Keefe said as he passed her a bottle. "Coca-Cola, it's the real thing, and don't forget things go better with Coke."

They sat down on the bench on Redmore's back stoop. The stoop was a social hub in warm weather, but the late-afternoon temperature was keeping today's customers from coming out to join them. The gossiping at Redmore's was likely to take place inside the store's warmth until spring.

"We finished pulling the turnips today, which is a good thing, since they were just about frozen solid in the ground. I thought my fingers would fall off when we got started just after sunup."

"Will you be leaving Fullerton's, then?"

"I'm not sure, but old man Fullerton said I could have tomorrow afternoon off. We have to bag all the turnips tomorrow, but he said if we get at it early enough in the morning and get done before lunch I could take the afternoon off."

"Let's finish our Cokes and get going. Mom's making pizza for supper."

"Piece of what?"

"You're funny. You've had pizza before, haven't you?"

"Can't say I have. I'm going to run back in the store and buy one of Mrs. Redmore's pies. Your mother feeds me all the time. You don't think she would mind if I bring her a pie, do you?"

"Of course she won't mind. She won't want you to spend your money, though."

"Would apple be okay?"

"Apple would be great."

*

Summer stood in the upstairs window watching the road, hoping the rain would not keep Keefe from biking up from Fullerton's this afternoon. Dad had wrestled the bike in the trunk last night so Keefe would have it to ride today. As long as the snow stayed away and as long as he was still at Fullerton's, biking to see her was a possibility. Just a bit of what he had told her last night about what it was like at his uncle's led Summer to believe she would not get to see him while he was there.

"I'll give your dad's bike back before I go to Uncle Tom's place."

"Why, do you think it's too far to bike from there to here?"

"No, it's not too far. He wouldn't let me keep the bike."

"He wouldn't think you stole it or something, would he? Dad could tell him he gave it to you."

"He'd be mad. He wouldn't want anyone to think I was a charity case."

"What if you told him you bought it?"

"He'd be mad about that too, and he'd likely sell it just to show me he's the boss."

Keefe had quickly changed the topic and there had been no more discussion about going to his uncle's house. During the evening Summer resisted the urge to show Keefe what she had purchased on her trip to town earlier in the day. She was waiting until he came the next afternoon before giving him the surprise.

"I want to make sure I see him coming, Mom," Summer hollered from the upstairs landing. "I want to be with him when he walks into the back porch and sees the stuff."

Last night while Don Barkley was driving Keefe back to Fullerton's, Summer and her mother had rearranged the back porch, setting up the easel and other art supplies Summer had bought at the art store on Prince William Street earlier in the day. The man had helped her choose the variety of art supplies, giving Keefe several choices on which medium he would use.

"What medium does your friend prefer?"

Medium was the word the salesman at the store had used, and he had to explain to Summer what it meant.

"He just uses a pencil," Summer answered, showing the man the two drawings Keefe had given her.

"Wow, he's good. He's never tried using charcoal or oil paints?"

"No. He just draws."

When Summer left the store, she had two large bags of supplies, three canvases, and a wooden easel. Her mom had offered to help pay and seemed as excited as Summer with the purchases.

"Keefe won't be happy that we spent so much because he won't be able to pay us back right now," Summer said as they put everything in the back seat.

"He can give us a bit at a time. I think it is terrible the boy doesn't have anyone who cares the least bit about him. Can you even imagine not having a family to love you and support the things you care about? I don't mind buying these things for him at all, and he's just going to have to let me. I want him to know he can come to our house to use them too. It doesn't seem like there is anywhere else he can keep them and get a chance to see what he can do with them."

"Thanks, Mom. This is really nice of you."

"He's coming!" Summer hollered now as she flew down the stairs, grabbed her raincoat off the hook by the back door, and ran up the driveway to meet Keefe Williams.

*

"Is that Keefe Williams turning in your driveway?" Nancy asked as the bus topped the hill and came to a stop at Summer's mailbox.

"Yes," Summer answered quickly, grabbing her book bag and heading to the front. As she stepped out onto the ground she could see several faces pressed against the bus window, her exit from the bus suddenly an event worth gawking at.

Keefe was standing halfway down the driveway waiting for Summer.

"Mr. Fullerton had to go to town and his wife said I could have the rest of the day off," Keefe called out. "I hope it's okay I came up this afternoon. I meant to get here before the bus came by."

"Of course it's okay."

"I don't want them to give you a hard time."

"Would you stop? I don't care who knows we're friends."

"Have you told anyone we've been spending time together?"

"No, it's nobody's business."

"I figured you wouldn't tell anyone. I guess I better enjoy it now, because once I go back to school you'll have to pretend you don't even know me."

"Why would I pretend I didn't know you?"

"Well, what's the reason you haven't told any of your new friends you're hanging out with me?"

"Why would I tell them? It's none of their business and I don't care what they think."

"Would you tell them if I was your boyfriend?"

"Are you my boyfriend?"

"Do you want me to be?"

"Listen. I'll tell everyone you're my friend, and when you get back to school I will not act any differently than I do now. You are a boy and you are my friend, a really good friend, so I guess that makes you my boyfriend. Let's stop wasting any more time talking about this. You can go work on the painting you started on the weekend and I'll get my homework done before supper."

*

Keefe got up from the table and started piling up the plates.

"Thank you. Supper was delicious, Mrs. Barkley. I'll help Summer with the dishes and you and Mr. Barkley can have your tea and relax."

"You are very welcome, Keefe. And I think it's time you start calling us Marilyn and Don. This Mr. and Mrs. stuff is not necessary," Marilyn Barkley said.

Keefe's face flushed.

"You are welcome in our home anytime. You can come here to paint whenever you want, you know."

"It was so nice of you to buy those supplies for me, Mrs. Barkley—I mean, Marilyn. I have two more dollars to give you."

"Don't even worry about it, Keefe," Don Barkley said.

"I won't come to paint unless you let me keep paying for the stuff you bought me. I don't think I'll be here for a while, though. I'm going to my uncle's tomorrow. I'll be back in school and I certainly won't have any free time after school."

"Well, hurry up and do the dishes so you can get back to work then," Marilyn Barkley said.

Summer began filling the dishpan as Keefe set the dirty dishes on the counter.

"Why didn't you tell me earlier you were going to your uncle's house tomorrow?"

"I don't know. Trying not to think about it, I guess."

"Do you know how long you'll be there?"

"No. He doesn't tell me anything. He'll have lots for me to do. He won't have put a stick of wood in the basement yet.

He'll keep me at least until I get the winter's wood in unless he gets a better offer for me. Let's just finish up these dishes. I want to show you what I did when you were upstairs. The waterfall painting is almost finished, I think. Do you want it when I'm done?"

"Sure. I still think you should show someone, though. I could take it to school and show Mr. Hartt. Maybe he'd let you do some painting at school if he knew how good you were."

"No. I'll go back to school and do what I always do. Mr. Wheaton will be glad to get Keefe Williams back. Heavy lifting, that's my claim to fame."

"Well, if you're giving your first painting to me, I'm going to get it framed and hang it on the living room wall. And I'm going to tell everyone it was painted by an artist named Keefe Williams."

*

Pink streamers and large accordion-folded red hearts decorated the gym. The lights had been dimmed a bit and Mr. McGuire had even allowed the decorating committee to hang strobe lights, transforming the gym into a romantic Valentine setting for February's junior high dance. Summer and Keefe were dancing slowly to Simon and Garfunkel's "Bridge over Troubled Water."

Summer had been true to her claim. She treated Keefe just the same when he returned to school and it was now an accepted fact: Summer Barkley and Keefe Williams were going steady. Keefe still took some ribbing, but for the most part his status had improved greatly. Even Winston Rideout realized dating the new girl was a game changer.

And Summer Barkley was not to be fooled around with. She was the editor for the school newspaper and quickly called attention in the weekly edition of *MCS Weekly Words* to any injustices she saw. She hadn't used names, but a write-up about a group of boys helping themselves to lunchboxes in the grade-seven coatroom had bought Mr. McGuire down heavy on the culprits. Winston and his friends now needed hall passes to leave the classroom, and most teachers weren't giving those out too freely.

Summer and Keefe made the best of their time together at school, as Keefe was still with his uncle. He did manage to call Summer almost every night, but there had only been a few times he could actually come to the Barkleys' to visit. Without the opportunity to use the art supplies at the Barkleys', Keefe had gone back to the pencil to fill up the sketchpads Marilyn Barkley had given him for Christmas.

Keefe told Summer very little of what went on under his uncle's roof, but Summer knew the last three months had been tough for him.

"I can't believe you walked all the way here tonight. It's freezing cold. You should have called. My dad would have gone to get you."

"I thought Uncle Tom was going to drive me up but at the last minute he said he wouldn't. I was so ticked off I just walked out the door and kept going. Mr. Smith picked me up just past Shamper's Bluff."

"You walked a long way. Dad will drive you home."

"*Home*. I wish."

When the music stopped, Keefe and Summer left the gym and sat down on a bench just outside. The beginning guitar riff of "American Woman" was booming from the open door. Keefe reached under the bench and pulled out his backpack. He unzipped it and pulled out a sketchpad.

"I've been going there," Keefe said. "I always wanted to, but I could never make myself."

Keefe passed the sketchpad to Summer. He started shaking as he glanced over at the pencil sketch Summer had opened to.

"Is this the house?"

"What's left of it."

"Oh, Keefe. I'm so sorry. You had never seen it before?"

"No. Crazy, eh? Almost sixteen years since it happened and I've been right next door all my life and I never walked over. I went a couple of weeks ago and I've been there every day since."

Summer turned to the next page, then flipped through the pad. "The whole pad is full. Are all the sketches from there?"

"Yes." Keefe took the sketchpad from Summer and opened to the last page. "This is what's left of the veranda. The gingerbread trim is still intact. I almost missed it. The corner was just sticking up through the snow."

"Keefe. These drawings are amazing, but they make me

feel so sad. It must have been hard for you to be there. You shouldn't have gone alone. I would have gone with you."

Summer wrapped her arms around Keefe, wishing she could take away the pain she saw in his eyes and in his sketches. She kissed Keefe's cheek.Mr. McGuire's booming voice made Summer jump. "What are you two lovebirds doing out here? Last dance and this shindig wraps up. You two better get in there and let the Carpenters sing the night out for you. This thing shuts down at nine. I've got a hockey game across the river at ten thirty."

Keefe quickly stuffed the sketchpad back into his backpack and slipped it under the bench. He certainly didn't want Mr. McGuire or anyone else to see the drawings on these pages. He would give the sketchpad to Summer to take home with her. He was anxious to get a chance to stand at the easel in Barkley's back porch and paint the one drawing in the book haunting him the most.

*

Walking down the overgrown path that had once been a driveway, Summer was unsure what to expect. The painting Keefe had started the day after the Valentine's dance was of the hill, or what remained of it, at least. Keefe had become overwhelmed with emotion as he tried to explain the half-finished painting to her.

"I want you to go there with me," Keefe said. "There are craters, deep gullies and roots, rocks, and of course what is left of the house. The barn and all the other outbuildings are still standing, the alders and bushes grown up around them. You won't even believe it unless you see it yourself. It is awful."

Keefe had broken down and sobbed leaving the porch, giving Summer the message he was done talking about it. Later he had taken the canvas off the easel and turned it toward the wall. He had not returned to the painting but had started painting the snow-covered orchard behind the Barkleys' house. He hadn't mentioned Summer coming with him to his parents' property again until they started walking there this dreary morning on the last day of March.

"I can't shake it. I wake up at night and see the mud. Why after all this time has it become so real to me?"

"You were a baby when it happened, Keefe. It makes sense you didn't think about it before now."

"It's weird, but a whole lot of things are coming to me. I think I stuffed it all down just to get by. I keep thinking about my cousin Elizabeth. It's her face I keep seeing when I wake up in the night. Elizabeth made me a birthday cake and it had five candles on it. I was in grade three when Elizabeth died. My aunt died then too."

"How did Elizabeth die?"

"I'm not sure."

Keefe stopped walking and faced Summer. "Last night when I woke up from my nightmare, I remembered a fight Uncle Tom and Elizabeth had. I woke up to her screaming and calling my uncle a murderer. She said he may as well have killed my parents with his own two hands and as long as she lived she would never forgive him."

*

Keefe tossed violently in the narrow bed under the eaves. The dream had been so real. He had been rushing up the hill toward his uncle, knee high in mud, screaming above the sound of the torrent. At the top, he could see his uncle in the plaid shirt he always wore, his faded Massey Ferguson hat tilted on his head. He was jeering, and despite the loudness of wind and rain, Keefe could hear his uncle's cruel laughter.

"You bastard," he screamed, fighting his way to the top of the hill. He woke just as he reached out for his uncle.

He pulled back the blankets and rose to his feet, reaching for his clothes on the chair beside the bed.

Tom, just waking from a restless sleep on the cot in the dim kitchen, slowly got to his feet. From the cold air in the kitchen he knew the fire had died down. Percy had left hours ago and the empty pint of rum they'd shared sat on top of the warming oven. Apparently, Percy had not thought to stock the fire up before he'd left. Tom took a stick of wood from the wood box and lifted the lid of the cook stove.

*

Marilyn Barkley set a birthday cake down in front of Keefe. "I hope you like chocolate cake with boiled frosting."

"Yes, thank you, Marilyn. It was really nice of you to make me a cake." Keefe's voice broke as he looked away. "Thanks for getting me out of that house."

A week ago Keefe had knocked at the Barkleys' back door shortly after midnight. He had a head wound requiring fourteen stitches, and after returning from the emergency department they got the story of what had happened out of Keefe.

Don Barkley pulled his chair away from the table and went to the cupboard to get cups for tea. "Your Uncle Tom came around to my way of thinking when I told him I was going to lay charges for assault and for the years of neglect and abuse if he didn't consent to us becoming your guardians. He knew his cash cow of renting out a minor to neighbours was not something Social Services would turn a blind eye to once they were informed. I can't believe no one questioned this before and I feel guilty for not doing anything earlier, Keefe."

"Don't worry about it. It wasn't always as bad as it was the other night. I'm sorry I got you guys involved."

"Are you kidding me, Keefe? He could have killed you," Summer said.

"Yeah, I got his dander up all right. He sure didn't like me accusing him of killing my parents."

Marilyn Barkley lit the sixteen candles. "Make a wish, Keefe."

Keefe stood to blow out the candles. "I don't know how to thank you for letting me live here. I'll do my share around here. And you can trust me with your daughter. I wouldn't do anything to mess things up. I love and respect your daughter."

"We are not worried, Keefe," Marilyn Barkley said. "We trust Summer to make good decisions. But I'm not saying Don won't be watching you like a hawk. His daughter is precious to him and he wouldn't even consider inviting you to live under the same roof if he thought he couldn't trust you."

"I can use your help around here for sure," Don Barkley interjected. "We'll give you an allowance so you can start putting some money away for your future. I don't expect free labour. I do expect you to be in school regularly, and I expect an improvement in your marks. I think having us on the backs of those teachers will help too. They haven't been doing their part. We are going to get you through MCS and then I think you should go to Vocational school instead of Hampton High. They have a good art program at Voc. Once you graduate you can go on to college and get some real art training."

Keefe sat staring at his cake, tears running down his cheeks. The caring and concern in Don's voice was overwhelming. These people acted like family. Earlier he'd been told to move his belongings into Hudson's old room and he knew what a big deal that was. Under this roof Keefe Williams was a person, someone who mattered, someone with a future. He would work hard and not let this opportunity be for nothing. He would prove he was someone worth believing in.

*

Marilyn turned off the kitchen light and started up the stairs to bed. It had been an emotional day starting with her early morning task of cleaning out Hudson's bedroom. It had taken a bit of convincing to get Don to go along with her idea to give Keefe Hudson's room.

"I can clean out the attic and set up a bed for him up there," Don said.

"It is still too cold up there."

Don had walked away and at first she thought it might be best to leave the discussion at that. She could approach him again later. Maybe it would be easier to just set a bed up for Keefe in the corner of the TV room for now. Don always closed Hudson's bedroom door if it was open when he walked by. Whenever she left it open it would be closed again shortly afterwards.

"I think it's time we faced his room," Marilyn said following her husband downstairs. "Cleaning it out and letting Keefe use it doesn't mean we're forgetting him. I'll do it if it's too hard for you, hon."

Don stopped and put his arms around his wife. "You're so strong. It's become too hard for me to even go by that room. At first I needed to sit in there surrounded by his books, his toys, and all the things he loved so much. Then after a while I just wanted to scoop everything up and take it to the garbage barrel and burn it. It is so hard looking at his treasures and knowing he is never coming back. But the other side of me wants to keep everything just the way it is, as if moving one thing would take him away from us in some final, unbearable way. I know cleaning it out is the right thing to do but *I* can't do it. I won't stop you from doing it though."

Don had left right after breakfast, using the excuse that he needed something in Hampton for the painting job he'd volunteered to do at the Baptist church. After watching him drive up the driveway, she'd gone right to Hudson's room.

As difficult as it had been to sort through Hudson's things and decide what to do with everything, she had not cried. Even when she rearranged the furniture and emptied the dresser drawers, she had not shed a tear. She had completely cleaned the room and got it ready for Keefe without giving in to the deep emotion of the task.

But as she'd stood mixing up the chocolate cake batter for Keefe's birthday cake, a flood of emotion came over her and she slumped to the kitchen floor, sobbing. The core of her grief was as raw and overwhelming as it had been in those first moments when standing in the emergency room she had been confronted with the unimaginable. No amount of time, no amount of change, and no amount of determination would ever alter the deep sorrow of losing her son.

By the time Don got home Marilyn was spreading the dollops of boiled icing on the cake. The redness of her tear-stained face had faded. She'd managed to clean out Hudson's room, get the room ready to welcome Keefe, prepare a birthday supper, and make her traditional birthday cake. Don thought she was so strong, so brave and so focused. Maybe she was some of that, but as she stood on the landing looking out at the moonlit sky she knew that whatever she had accomplished since that terrible moment and whatever she managed to do in the future, that grief would never be any less or the loss any easier to bear.

Summer and Keefe sat in the TV room, neither one of them paying the least bit of attention to the *Columbo* episode on the screen.

"I didn't mean to act like a crybaby at suppertime," Keefe said.

"No one thought you were being a crybaby. I'm just glad you were here for your birthday, and I'm so glad you trust Mom and Dad enough to let them help you. None of this is your fault, you know. Your uncle needs to answer for the way he has treated you," Summer said, kissing Keefe's cheek. "I love you, Keefe Williams. I think you are the bravest person I know."

"Oh, I'm brave, all right. I let the old bastard treat me like shit all these years. I never even talked back to him. He would have got the worst end of the fight though if he hadn't grabbed the poker. Scared the shit out of him when he saw how much blood there was. He put me in the car and drove me here. I think he was afraid I was going to call the police."

*

Don watched Keefe pull the stepladder from the back of

his new Dodge truck. Since he started Peninsula Drywall Company three years ago, Keefe worked with him quite often. Getting jobs drywalling, crack filling, and painting hadn't been hard once he'd put his shingle out. Concentrating on his new business and putting so much energy into the boy had been good for him, even though Marilyn worried he might be focusing on Keefe to keep from dealing with his feelings. He was not using Keefe to replace Hudson. How could helping Keefe succeed take anything away from his love for his son? If anything, it gave him something to care about, which in the long run helped him be a better father to Summer and a better husband to Marilyn.

Marilyn had her own struggles. She focused on feeding them all, creating a comfortable home, and working in her gardens. She also went regularly to a support group for parents who had lost a child. That was not something he was interested in doing. He had found being here in the solitude of his boyhood home and staying busy was the type of comfort he needed. He was not the least bit interested in commiserating with other parents.

Keefe was a good kid, and Don hadn't for one minute regretted having him come to live with them. His only concern was that having Keefe as a part of the family might makes things difficult for Summer if she realized Keefe wasn't the young man she wanted to spend her life with. Their relationship certainly seemed serious for both right now. But what if that changed?

Don shifted the heavy pail of crack-fill compound to his other hand. For now he would have to let that worry go. Keefe was doing well in high school. He had a home for the first time and a family who cared about him. If the relationship between Summer and Keefe changed in the future, they would figure it out. Don knew just how quickly life can throw a curveball, but he also knew that even in the midst of the unthinkable, some force keeps you going.

*

Summer straightened the mortarboard on Keefe's head. "I know you think this is stupid, but did you really think Mom and Dad were going to let you get away with not going to your high school graduation? And don't even pretend you aren't excited about the award you're getting and the scholarship. It's a good thing the Hampton High and Vocational School graduations aren't on the same night, because I honestly think Mom and Dad would choose yours over mine. They are so proud of you."

"You didn't do so shabby in the scholarship department yourself, Summer Barkley. Not sure how we're going to manage being apart from each other next year."

"We'll see each other at Thanksgiving, Christmas, and summer holidays."

"If I had my way I'd marry you right now and follow you to Queen's. I could get a job and just paint on my own without a fancy art degree. I could always go to school once you were done."

"As tempting as marrying you sounds, my parents would not go for it at all. They want both of us educated. You are not throwing away your future just to put a ring on my finger. We have lots of time to get married. Now hurry up. They're lining up for the procession. I'm proud of you, Keefe."

Summer heard the sobbing when she opened the washroom door. The sound of her mother weeping was rare, but when it happened it still ripped Summer's heart out. Sometimes an occasional tear would drop on her mother's cheek or she'd see Dad bat a tear from his eye, as if allowing it to drop would be to give in to the sadness they all dealt with every day. Birthdays, Christmases, and other occasions so difficult to face without Hudson came and went, but for the most part nobody cried.

Summer ducked into a cubicle, quickly deciding not to let Mom know she was in the washroom. She would let Mom have her moment. The energy and attention Mom had given to her and Keefe's graduation year had been extreme. She'd had a constant smile on her face for weeks, but the sorrow of never having the joy of Hudson's milestones was always there for all of them.

*

Summer slipped into the row beside her parents.

"All Keefe's paintings are on display in the library," Marilyn Barkley said. "A reporter interviewed us before we came in to sit down. They are doing a piece on him in tomorrow's paper."

"I don't know how happy Keefe is going to be about the publicity, but as far as I'm concerned it's about time more people recognized his talent," Summer whispered.

"Well, if it isn't the celebrity," Winston Rideout jeered as Summer and Keefe walked into Kingston Store two days later. "An artist. What did you use Williams, paint-by-number? It was quite the picture of you in the paper. Big high school graduate! Aren't you a big deal?"

"He is a big deal, Winston. When's *your* graduation?" Summer said, edging her way between Keefe and Winston.

"Oh, shut up. I never had your parents swoop in and pay the teachers to pass me. Some of us had to quit school and get jobs. I didn't have some bleeding heart take pity on me. Rideouts don't take charity."

Keefe stood glaring at Winston Rideout. He wanted so badly to punch him in the face, but if he let Winston's words get to him he might not be able to stop at one punch. All the years of Winston's bullying and every other injustice Keefe had felt would boil over, and he wasn't sure he could contain it. Punching this jerk would not take the hurt away. Keefe knew the only way to overcome his pain was the way he had chosen on the night five years ago when he sat at the Barkley's table on his sixteenth birthday. Hard work, his art, and the motivation of making Summer and her parents proud of him were all he cared about.

"Do you want Coke or 7 Up, Summer?" Keefe asked as he opened the pop cooler.

*

"I'm going to take my portfolio from school, but I'm leaving these here if your mother doesn't mind storing them for me," Keefe said as he set the canvases aside and began packing the items on his work table into a cardboard box.

"Don't you think you might get back to these if you took them with you?" asked Summer, picking up a canvas. "I think the first three you did are amazing."

"I'm going to put it all out of my mind. I've spent my whole life in the shadow of what happened to my parents. I was robbed of a childhood and a family by a rainstorm and a greedy uncle who didn't admit his actions caused their death. Instead of facing any responsibility for what happened, he made it his mission to punish me for surviving. I cannot even begin to get back what he took from me, but I can move on. I can leave this place and never look back. I have done all the searching I care to do. Nobody can tell me what really happened, and even if someone told me my uncle's clearcutting caused the mudslide, what good would it do me? I have laid my parents and Elizabeth to rest. The only people I care about on this peninsula are you and your parents. I am going to find my future somewhere else, and I hope you are willing to as well. Of course, we'll visit your parents, but I am not going to live the rest of my life and bring a family up in the place where I was treated like a freak because of the way my parents died.

Keefe took the canvas from Summer. "I have sketched every square inch of my parents' property. I had to draw every trace of what was left after the destruction. But I'm done. The land can sit there, and every board of the house, the barn, and the sheds can rot back into the earth. My scholarship to OCAD can pay my way out of here. But I want your parents to hang this one on the living room wall to remember and honour my mother. Her final act of love saved my life."

Keefe set the canvas on the easel and stepped back to look at the painting. The painting was of a veranda roof, each detail precise and impeccable, its structure still intact, and if one viewed it in isolation one could imagine it attached to a stately home as part of an attractive landscape. It was collapsed, though, nearly sunken in the earth and surrounded by a landscape of destruction: gullies of mud, rocks of all sizes, upturned roots, and the splintered remains of a house no longer standing.

PART TWO
1989

Summer set Keefe's cup of coffee down on the window ledge.

"What's the occasion? It's not every morning my wife delivers coffee to my studio," Keefe said. "I thought once you got to your office for the day, nothing short of a call from the kids' school got you out. And even in that case a broken limb would be the only call to rate."

"Oh, stop it. I went to get Melanie when she threw up in grade one."

"I think the teacher had to describe the chunks to you before you actually went to pick her up."

"Would you stop? Do you want to have coffee with me or not? I can leave you alone if you want."

"No, stay. But to what do I owe this pleasure?"

"I've been thinking."

"Oh, that's not good."

"Can I tell you or not?"

"Yes, of course you can."

"You aren't going to be happy about what I'm going to say."

"Really." Keefe set his paintbrush down and took his coffee off the windowsill. "I may as well sit down and give you my undivided attention. If you've stopped writing long enough to come in here it must be important, so you may as well just come out with it."

"I can't seem to get to work on the book Scholastic has contracted me to write. I've been putting those easy readers out one right after the other, but I can't settle down and write this one."

"Don't tell me the well has run dry. Those books are the cash cow right now and allow this artist to live the dream. God knows the few paintings I sell wouldn't support this family. What is standing in your way, my beautiful wordsmith?"

"Another book is getting in the way. You won't like it when I tell you what it is, but I can't shake it. I've even started it, although I won't keep working on it unless you tell me I can."

"What are you talking about? Since when do you need my permission to write something? You have never tried to tell me what to paint. God knows if you did I might sell more paintings."

"Keefe, I'm being serious. The story I can't stop thinking about is yours. I've always had the feeling I needed to write it, but I've felt that need even stronger since last summer at Mom and Dad's after Zac asked you to show him where you lived when you were little. Your answer broke my heart, Keefe. You are a grown man with two children of your own. You are a talented artist and a wonderful man, but you are still an orphaned baby, a hurt little boy, and a lonely, sad teenager."

Summer looked at Keefe's face, trying to read his expression and waiting for a response. Silence prompted her to continue.

"I could say you need to paint your story, but I won't. Someday you might or you might not. But I want to write it. I want to know more. I want you to know more. I want you to finally put the pain of it away and find the truth in what happened to you. I think you ran away from the pain. I really want to do this, but I won't do it if you ask me not to."

Keefe got up and walked across his studio to the large window. This view of Georgian Bay was the sight he allowed to fill his soul every morning. It was his chosen home, and he was so thankful for what he and Summer had built here together. They had planted the two linden trees on the lawn, one when Zachary Hudson Williams was born nine years ago and the other when Melanie Vera Williams was born seven years ago. Summer and his two kids were his life and this was his home.

He was so thankful for this place. But every day a part of him mourned and longed for another place. He felt like his chosen exile had been necessary but the sorrow of it remained. Last summer's visit to the peninsula had been difficult. His reaction to his son's request to see where he'd lived as a little boy had taken him by surprise. He had felt a deep sadness mixed with shame and a desperate need to hide his past from his son. Why had it caused him such anguish after all this time?

"The house isn't there anymore, Zac. There's nothing there to show you. This house was my first real home. I had no family until I met your mother and Grammie and Grampie."

He had left the room after answering Zachary, walked down to the beach, and sobbed like a baby.

Keefe stood at the window, reluctant to voice his thoughts. Summer often challenged him about his refusal to face his pain, but she had spent years doing exactly the same thing. She told other stories to keep from looking at her own. She never talked about the day her brother died and she certainly never acknowledged how much pressure she put on herself to be worthy of being the one her parents were left with.

Keefe walked back over and sat down beside his wife. "You can write it if you want. I can't tell you much more than I already have. If you want to write about the shitty childhood I had I can tell you what I remember, but I don't know what good it would do either of us. You *were* my first family, you know. You were the first person who ever saw me. But go ahead and write whatever you must. I trust you, Sum. Go ahead and tell it."

Summer cradled Keefe's head on her shoulder, accepting the tears he was allowing her to see.

"You should write to Gladys Titus," Keefe said after a few minutes of silence. "She was my mother's best friend. She was the only one who ever told me anything about my mother. Every time I saw her when I was growing up, she would tell me how much my mother loved me. Could you thank her for that?"

*

Back in her office a few minutes later, Summer brought up the familiar page on her computer. How long ago had she written the prologue for the book that had been pulsating in her brain since last summer? The book had been nagging at her a lot longer ago than that. She remembered the day her dad had taken such care and precision to hang the framed painting Keefe had asked to be hung in her parents' living room as a tribute to his mother. Later that night Summer had frantically written in a brand-new journal all the thoughts flooding her mind, remembering Keefe's reaction to the painting being hung. She had written every bit of information Keefe had shared, every rumour she'd heard, every bit of anything she knew about Keefe's story. And over the years she had added to it.

Prologue

Every community has thousands of stories that take place in the lifespan of one person. Some are small and incidental and perhaps only a few people remember them. Some have more magnitude and reverberate for decades before the remnants die down and fade. Sometimes one or two people seem to remember every incident. Maybe they remember what they were wearing or what they were doing and who they got a ride from the ferry with on the day it happened. Maybe these memories are accurate, or maybe they have taken on qualities far from the truth and if the teller were to be transported right back to the day, the week, or the season when the happening was brand new and on the lips and minds of everyone, the facts would conflict with the story that has taken shape.

The stories of a place come in all descriptions. An affair, quietly taking place for twenty years. A soldier bean swallowed and swelling, taking the life's breath of a toddler, leaving mothers for the next ten years solemnly warning their offspring about the dangers of baking beans. Fatal house fires, some so memorable the site still haunts the people who stood below, urging the man to jump to safety. Certain places along the winding roads where people travel every day, where accidents took place and lives were lost. Pockets of people remember the one in the Wallace woods or the one on the Centreton or the one just past Tom Brown's hill. The drowning of a young mother trying to save a child's life and losing her own. The fall from a barn loft, breaking a man's neck. The accidents resulting in lost fingers or crippled legs. The unsolved mystery of a young man who left his house and vanished early one morning.

Someone should write these things down you often hear. But where would a person start? Where would a person start, and what if this person was from away?

Being from away is not a cut-and-dry assessment. It can be a person who just moved to the area yesterday or someone who came at the beginning of grade seven. Or she might be a "summer person," which doesn't quite cut it because the days don't add up when you're counting years of just Julys and Augusts. How long must a person live somewhere to be from a place? The criteria can sometimes be very stringent.

Being a writer in a small community is presumptuous enough, but when you start to search out one of its most entrenched stories, you are bound to get somebody's dander up. But the only person I ever really cared about when telling this story was Keefe, and if he doesn't mind me telling the story, no one else should. It is his story, or as he used to call it, "the damn story," and the only thing anyone ever thought about when they looked at him. He was the baby who survived when the hill came down.

Through tear-filled eyes, Summer brought up a blank page and began writing a letter to Gladys Titus.

*

"Does she know what happened to my cousin Elizabeth?" Keefe asked.

Summer had been writing letters back and forth to Gladys, and at first Keefe acted as if he was not interested in hearing what the woman was writing back to her. But two weeks ago, he had asked Summer to specifically ask her about his cousin. He was surprised at what he was remembering, and more surprised that he was sharing the details with Summer.

"My first memory of Elizabeth was when I was around four years old, I think. I remember the crib, the cage she got me out of."

"What do you mean, cage?" Summer asked.

"I slept in a crib in the little room off the kitchen. It's a bathroom now, but when I was little they kept me there. The crib had a wire frame across the top so I couldn't get out. I remember Elizabeth opening the wire top and getting me out. She dragged the crib outside and I never slept in that room again."

"That's terrible, Keefe. I remember once you told me you didn't talk until you were four. Not much wonder, if they kept you in a cage. Why were they such monsters?"

"I have no idea. My aunt was always sick in her room as I recall. My uncle was mean and hollered all the time. After Elizabeth came she looked after me, so I didn't really pay much attention to them."

*

Summer took the letter from the envelope, skimming through the first page before finding the paragraph Gladys had written telling what she knew about Elizabeth. Summer read the passage aloud to Keefe.

I have not thought about Elizabeth Rogers for a long time. I feel terrible now when I think of what Keefe went through and that I did nothing to prevent it. I should have stepped in and done more, but Tom and Helen made it perfectly clear I had no business sticking my nose in when I tried to get involved after Elizabeth went to the hospital. I knew Elizabeth was having a very difficult time in the months after Vera and Jud's deaths, but until her breakdown I thought she was managing. Helen was not forthcoming at the time about Elizabeth's condition and she did not welcome any of my inquiries during the years Elizabeth was gone.

When Elizabeth finally came back she seemed well. She treated Keefe as if he were her own. I remember seeing her the day he started grade one, and she was so proud of him. She was working at the diner by the ferry, trying to save money so they could get a place of their own. It was tragic what happened to the dear girl. I can't even imagine what drove her to such desperation. Her mother died shortly afterwards. I am sure it was more than Helen could live with, knowing her daughter had taken her own life.

"She killed herself," Keefe said. "I must have heard someone say that when I was a kid, because I remember being so angry at her for leaving me. I couldn't understand how she could have left me on purpose. It was shortly after Elizabeth died that my uncle started farming me out. After my aunt died, I guess. It never mattered to me where he sent me; any place was better than being with him."

"What a terrible man he is. Do you ever feel like you need to have it out with him, confront him about the terrible way he treated you?"

"He's an old man; a miserable old man. I would not waste my energy facing off with him. He is absolutely nothing to me."

"I am not going to say you should or shouldn't confront him, but I do believe he owes you something. Maybe you'll never get an apology or any admission of guilt from him about any of what he did, but I think he should be forced to take some responsibility."

"I will not give him the satisfaction of knowing how much he hurt me. If I shut him out completely, he can't hurt me anymore."

"I don't know if I believe you or not. But it is not for me to say."

Summer skimmed the remainder of Gladys's letter as Keefe returned to his easel, indicating the discussion about confronting his uncle was over.

Please tell your husband how much his parents loved him and how thrilled they were when he was born. His mother chose his name because it means *cherished*. Vera would have cherished and adored her son and the life he would have had under his parents' roof would have been very different from the one he had. I hope knowing that gives him some comfort. Both his parents were wonderful people and I miss them every day.

"Cherished." Keefe took the letter from his wife and reread the paragraph she had just read to him. "Cherished," he repeated.

Keefe walked across the room and opened the cupboard, removing a large cardboard folder. He knelt to the floor and opened the folder, lifting out the canvases.

"I have never finished these because I thought I didn't need to. I thought I could let it go and move on. I thought painting my past would tie me to it. But you know, I never thought about painting these for them. Everything they loved was taken from them, and she released the baby she cherished as her final act of love. I am a grown man now, and it is time I thought about them, not myself. The lives of Vera and Jud Williams mattered. They deserve to have their story told, their legacy honoured and remembered. I do not need to say my piece to an uncle who disrespected their memory by treating their son in the way he did. I need to respect and value their memory and right the wrong myself. His hatred is nothing when put beside my parents' love. Celebrating their love will be my victory."

*

The first painting Keefe completed was entitled "Behold a Pale Horse." It took him two months and he worked at nothing else. Long days in his studio often resulted in only an hour or two of actual painting. Not a lot of painting but lots of remembering accompanied the first painting in a series Keefe was determined to create in the attempt to tell his parents' stories. After a day in the studio he would talk at length about whatever he had conjured up from his long-suppressed memories.

"The first place I remember going to work was a turkey farm. The man who owned it used to talk a lot about my father. 'You're a chip off the old block, you are, Keith,' he always said. I never corrected him. 'Your father and I were best buds growing up. He was the best turkey jerker around. The rest of us would tire, but he always made a game of it. A hard worker, your dad was. He could fix anything, you know. My old man used to say, "If Jud Williams can't fix it you may as well throw it in the scrap heap." He fell hard for your mother. She was a looker.'

"I had to work really hard at Gorham's, but I was always glad when I got sent back there because Mr. Gorham would always say the same things about my dad. *Chip off the old block.* I loved the way he said it. My uncle used to say something similar, but always in a mean way. 'You're just like your old man,' he would say, spitting the words out as if it were the worst thing he could possibly say about me.

"Could you ask Gladys what she remembers about the house? I want to paint it the way it was before it was destroyed. When I think of my parents' life, the house was such an important part of it. My aunt used to have rants, constantly criticizing Elizabeth, and she always said something nasty about Vera's house. When I was really young I didn't even know who Vera was, but as I got older I figured out she was talking about my mother's house. She would go into long tirades, saying things like if it was Vera's floor Elizabeth would wax it until it shone, if they were Vera's windows Elizabeth would keep them sparkling. She always spoke about Vera's house with such hatred and anger."

*

Four weeks later, Summer received several photographs of the house from Gladys, some showing the house in several stages of construction. One was of Vera Williams painting the gingerbread trim on the newly constructed front veranda. Keefe studied the photograph, his eyes filling with tears.

"That is the first picture I have ever seen of my mother. At least, I think it is. There used to be a wedding picture on Elizabeth's dresser. I looked for it after Elizabeth died, but I never saw it again."

"Gladys said your mother worked to help your father build the house. She is trying to find more photographs for you. She thinks Bill Henderson might have some, because he did up the plans for your parents and took a lot of pictures of it when it was completed. It was well built, she said, which made the way it was demolished even harder to believe. Listen to this." Summer pulled the letter out.

Vera loved her house, and it was certainly one of the nicest homes around at the time. Vera was not the type to brag or put on airs about it, though. She and Jud worked hard for the lovely home they had. They lived with Vera's parents for the first years of their marriage while saving to build it. When they moved in, we had a housewarming for them. Everyone came out and it was quite a night, but Helen and Tom didn't come. Their absence was so obvious and it hurt Vera a lot. Helen was always so jealous of Vera.

I am sending all the photographs I could find. I have also enclosed Vera's recipe for her famous brown bread. It is written in Vera's own hand. Vera had lovely penmanship.

Summer had been writing back and forth to Gladys for months, trying to get a picture of the early years of Vera and Jud Williams's marriage. Gladys had also given Summer an address for Keefe's cousin Margaret, and it turned out she lived only an hour's drive away. Keefe was not interested in meeting with her, but Summer made several visits to see the woman.

"Elizabeth's first breakdown came when my father shot my uncle's horse," Margaret shared on the first visit. "I had only talked to Elizabeth on the phone during the months after my aunt and uncle died. I didn't even come home for the funeral. I was very pregnant with my son Jason and I couldn't travel. She seemed all right whenever we spoke, but when I think back I know I didn't let myself consider how difficult it must have been for her. They were like parents to Elizabeth. I should have offered to have her and Keefe come to live with us.

"My mother called me to tell me when they took Elizabeth to the hospital," Margaret continued. "Mother said she had tried to kill our father. She had picked up the gun and pointed it at Dad before collapsing.

"Mother told me they had hired someone to help look after the baby while Elizabeth was in the hospital. I had no idea how Keefe was being treated. I know it's terrible that I never went down to see Elizabeth in the hospital or to visit my parents, but you have to understand the relationship I had with my parents. I was perfectly content to pretend things were fine so I could live my life away from them. I was completely in denial of what was going on, and it worked for me. When Elizabeth got home she called me, telling me what she found. I knew Mother was not well, but I didn't know how terrible things were for that little boy. I could not believe my parents had done such a thing.

"I came down for Elizabeth and stayed long enough to make sure she was able to manage and then visited a few times. The children and I were there for Keefe's fifth birthday. By then he was a normal, happy little boy. Elizabeth had done wonders with him."

"What about after Elizabeth died? Didn't you think you should have taken Keefe then?"

"It all happened so fast. I was still in shock from the fact Elizabeth had killed herself, and then a week later Mother was dead. I didn't come home. I know it sounds terribly selfish of me, but Gerald was concerned about my well-being. The children needed a strong mother and I was completely over-whelmed with the situation. Father told me Keefe was going to a couple in Gorham's Bluff, and I assumed at the time he was being adopted."

"You know your father rented Keefe out to people looking for cheap labour. He was eight years old working like a grown man. His schooling was sporadic and he had no childhood."

"I feel terrible. I really do. And I blame myself for not doing more to help Elizabeth. I should have insisted they come live with me. I live with the guilt every day. My parents made such a mess of us all. Henry and I aren't close. When I think of how desperately my aunt wanted a family and of how my parents completely ruined the one they were given, it breaks my heart. I have put all my energy into building a home for my children. This is probably hard for you to understand, but it is the only excuse I can offer for ignoring what Elizabeth and Keefe went through."

*

"Her name was Dolly," Summer told Keefe. "Your father bought her in Sussex before they started building the house. Gladys told me how angry your mother was at first when he bought her. But by the end of it she loved her and treated

Dolly like a pet. Gladys said afterwards Dolly wouldn't let anyone get near her. She had busted her way out of the barn and stood bawling for days after your parents died. They finally got her back in the pasture and left the door to the barn open, but she wouldn't even let the man who came to feed and water her in the months afterward near enough to touch her.

"Gladys's husband came to get the horse after your uncle shot her. He said she was a damn fine horse. Apparently, he always said the old bastard shot her for spite. Tom thought he could load her onto the trailer and sell her, but she would have none of it. She went down fighting, though, and gave Tom Rogers a nasty gash on his leg before he got the second shot into her.

"Poor Elizabeth came upon it and snapped," Summer added. "If there had been another bullet in the shotgun, she might have killed your uncle that morning."

"That would have changed things. If she had killed him, she would probably still be alive, and my life would have been a whole lot better. I wish the horse had kicked him in the head instead. One good, well-placed kick could have changed it all."

Keefe completed the next six paintings quite quickly. The one Summer found the most moving was of a detailed view of one wall of a pantry. Keefe had spent hours on small details like the labels of canned goods on one shelf, and the items on the work surface. The realistic bag of flour, the bread dough, and the utensils on the bread board were amazing. You could even read the ingredients listed for "Vera's Brown Bread" on the recipe card propped up on the first shelf.

"My aunt Helen had a pantry, but I was not allowed in it when Elizabeth wasn't home. One day when Elizabeth was at work I looked in my aunt's room and, thinking she was asleep, I tiptoed downstairs and snuck into the pantry. I climbed up on the wooden stool and was just reaching for a box of soda crackers when I felt my aunt's hand. She knocked me right off the stool. I hit my head on the edge of the counter, but I did not cry. I was not going to give her the satisfaction. I went upstairs and stayed in Elizabeth's room for the rest of the day until she got home. As I helped Elizabeth set the table for supper that night, my aunt went into great detail, telling Elizabeth about the two bowls of Campbell's tomato soup I had eaten at lunchtime.

"'He ate a whole sleeve of crackers with his soup,' she said, waving the box of crackers in front of me, daring me to say anything different.

"I think Elizabeth figured out Aunt Helen wasn't feeding me while she was at work, though, because I remember she would leave me a packed lunch in the porch. I was pretty much allowed to go wherever I liked when Elizabeth was at work if I stayed out of my aunt and uncle's way. I think I started drawing then. I would sit outside no matter what the weather and sketch on whatever paper I could find. I would show them to Elizabeth when she came home. She kept them in a box under her bed. She bought me my first sketchpads. I remember when I filled the last page of the final one after she died, I cried because I knew no one else would ever buy me another one.

"Not until you came along, anyway."

"This one is beautiful, Keefe. I love how you put the horse in the pasture beside the barn."

"I put Dad's truck in the driveway too. It's just like the one in one of the photographs Mrs. Titus sent. I don't even know for sure if it was Dad's truck, but in my imagination, it is. Mr. Gorham said he could fix anything. Wish he was around to fix the Cherokee. I think we're going to have to break down and buy a new vehicle."

"I can't see that happening anytime soon. But if we cared about driving new cars, we wouldn't be doing what we're doing for a living."

*

Summer hung up the phone from her conversation with her mother feeling somewhat perplexed and irritated. Normally when they discussed any hitches in her writing, her mom had a way of putting things in perspective and could help her get back on track. Summer was so thankful for the relationship she had with her mother, both personally and professionally. She knew it was a rare treasure, and she truly appreciated her mother's ability to see the whole picture. But her mother's words this morning had not been welcome.

"Perhaps you need to look at this from more than just Keefe's side. It is possible Tom Rogers's side is important to the truth? And maybe there is more to Helen's illness. There are few real monsters, you know, Summer. Everyone has a reason, some motivation causing them to act in a certain way. Maybe you need to dig a bit to really get the whole story."

Firstly, Summer thought, she had no interest in Tom Rogers's side of the story. What motivation could possibly justify the way he had treated Keefe and his own children? She certainly was not interested in sitting down and having a heart-to-heart with Tom. Margaret had not been there for much of what happened during those years, and Summer had no contact with Henry. Who was there she could even talk to, to get a perspective on whatever Tom's side of the story was? Did he even deserve to have his side regarded?

Summer returned to her office, mulling these thoughts over. She would let what her mother said sit awhile before deciding if and how she could delve into this mess. She certainly was not going to bring it up to Keefe. She could only imagine his reaction if she were to suggest his uncle had a place in the telling of this story. And Keefe might disagree with his mother-in-law's statement about monsters. Summer was quite sure Keefe would put his uncle and his aunt in the monster category, and no matter what the motivation or reasons behind their actions, the end results were unforgivable.

*

Two weeks later Summer looked at the notes in front of her. By this time, she and Gladys had gone from letters to regular phone calls. Sometimes Summer would call Gladys just to ask a quick question or clarify a small detail. How would a person find out about a major world event in the 1930s? Would they hear it on the radio or days later by mail or newspaper? Who owned the store in 1944? Her question two weeks ago had been, "Does Tom Rogers have any close friends?"

Gladys said, "If Tom ever had a friend, it was the almighty dollar," but after a few minutes she gave Summer the names of two men. "Dave Evans and Percy Johnston worked with Tom Rogers for years. I suppose they must be friends of some kind to have stuck around. It's not many would put up with him."

Summer used the trip home for her father's sixty-fifth birthday as an opportunity to meet with Dave Evans and Percy Johnston. She told Keefe she was meeting with a couple of neighbours to conduct a bit of research. Keefe stayed home with the children and she flew to New Brunswick for a quick weekend trip.

Summer spoke to Percy Johnston first. It surprised her how vivid his recollections were. She was also surprised his recollections held such emotion.

"I found your husband, you know," Percy said. "He was not even crying. Not a sound, even when I picked him up. It was a blue blanket, one of those thick ones with satin around them. Kenwood blanket, I think they're called. The wife and I got several for wedding gifts. I picked the little fella up and he stared into my eyes. Didn't even whimper. Glad to hear he grew up to be all right. I always wondered if the fall affected him. God love the little guy."

Percy didn't offer much about Tom Rogers. Summer kept trying to bring the discussion around to him, but Percy seemed more stuck on telling her about the morning after Keefe's parents died and his memories of the tragedy. Basically, all her notes from their conversation just added to what she had already pieced together and gave more clarity to what she already knew.

Dave Evans had a lot more to say about Tom Rogers. Summer didn't have to prompt him much to get the information that filled several pages of her notebook.

"I know a lot of folks don't like Tom Rogers," said Dave with a shrug, "but I never minded him. He doesn't have a chick nor child now. I go 'round and see him quite regular, even though I don't work with him anymore. He and I worked together for almost fifty years, so I guess it's kind of a habit for me to end up at his place. Now I know your husband wouldn't have no love lost for the man. He was rough on the kid. Rough on his own kids too. He is rough around the edges for sure, and this whole peninsula thinks Tom Rogers is the devil. They didn't think that when they took advantage of the young fella, though, did they? It always pissed me off afterwards when I would hear some of those same men talking about Tom after your folks took the Williams boy in. I never heard them with their high-and-mighty opinions when they were getting work out of the boy just by feeding him and putting a roof over his head. I know times have changed, but you can't tell me some of those men didn't treat their own kids about the same way they accused Tom of treating the Williams boy.

"But one thing I will tell you is Tom Rogers loved Helen. He was a good husband to that woman, and I sure wouldn't have been as patient with her as he was. He was real protective of her. She was not right in the head. My wife says she was always loopy, but I can't say. What I do know is Tom catered to her every desire. He would have done anything to keep her happy, and believe me, keeping her happy was not an easy task.

"Right jealous of everyone, she was, especially her sister. Nothing was good enough for her. Tom tried his best, bent over backwards, but it was never enough to keep Helen happy. She was a miserable woman. I'd have put a pillow over her head, I think, but Tom never lost his patience with her. He was mighty shaken when she died, I can tell you. Terrible thing to lose his daughter and his wife so close together. People can say what they want, but he's suffered, no doubt about it."

After their conversation Summer thought a lot about what Mr. Evans had told her, and now, reading his comments, she thought again about what her mother said that started this exploration. Motivation, reasons for doing what one does. *We all have them,* Summer thought. What were her reasons for writing this story? What was the motivation for Keefe to paint the paintings—now totalling fifteen—in the series he was creating to tell his parents' story? Somehow Dave Evan's words were chiselling a small crack in her solid shell of belief that Tom Rogers had no side to his story. Before this she hadn't had one shred of concern for him and no interest in seeing him as anything but a heartless, uncaring man who treated his nephew and his own children so horribly.

Summer didn't know where exactly to turn next, but she did know she needed to learn more about Helen Rogers and the power she seemed to have had over her husband. Keefe didn't talk much about his aunt, but any memories he shared were brutal. Helen Rogers had been erratic, physically abusive, and manipulative. It appeared this woman who had spent most of her adult life closeted away in her room had created an atmosphere of misery that had caused much of what happened. Had Tom Rogers, who at first glance seemed to be the bad guy, been swept along in the mess and not been completely to blame? If this were the case, maybe his side did warrant telling if the complete truth was to be told.

*

Tom Rogers opened the door a crack and stood in the dim shadow. He looked as if the knock may have woken him up. His dishevelled white hair and mottled beard gave him a comical appearance. He was stooped and shaky. The colourful striped suspenders holding up his faded baggy pants appeared clownlike. He did not look the least bit threatening and not the man Summer expected to see.

Susan White

"Mr. Rogers. I'm Summer Williams. I was wondering if I could talk to you about some things."

"Williams? There's no Williams around anymore. Where you from?"

"I am your nephew's wife. May I come in?"

"Oh. Is he back here? I thought he was out west or Ontario somewhere."

"Yes, we live in Ontario. Thornbury. Do you have a few minutes we could talk?"

"Oh, I've got all the time in the world. Do I look like a busy man? I'm lucky these days if I get out of bed or off the damn couch."

"So you don't mind if I come in?"

"Sure, come on in. Can't think what you want to talk to me about. I'm sure your husband and just about anybody you talk to around here has told you what a bastard I am. You want to hear it from the horse's mouth, do ya'? The horse. May as well start with the horse. Not much else I could have done with the old hag. She sure as hell wasn't letting me near her."

Summer followed Tom Rogers in through the front hall and into a small sitting room. The room was dark and cluttered with old furniture: a faded couch and matching armchair, a large roll-top desk, several end tables, and a fern stand holding a pot with a petrified plant, everything covered with a thick coat of dust. Tom turned the lamp on and moved a pile of newspapers off the armchair, gesturing for Summer to sit down.

"I could put the kettle on for tea, but I'm not sure I've got a clean cup to offer you. I'm not much of a housekeeper, but I guess you've probably already figured that out."

"No, I'm fine, thanks. I don't want you to go to any trouble. I'll get right to the point. I'm a writer. I'm writing my husband's story. This is awkward, and I'm not sure exactly why I'm here. I just thought you might want to have a say about things."

"A writer. Seems to me someone told me Keefe's wife wrote books. You talked to Dave and Percy the other day, didn't you? Bet you were scared to come here. Suppose you thought I'd send you packing. Everybody thinks I'm a mean son of a bitch. Never tried to convince them otherwise. What would be the point? The whole peninsula figures they know the whole story and I'm the bad guy. I must say, I'm surprised you of all people care about hearing anything I might have to say. I'm glad your parents did what they did for the boy. I'm glad he got away from here when he did. I could have killed him. Don't know what came over me. I'm not a bad man."

Summer looked over at the old man sitting across the room from her. Tears were filling his eyes and one dropped onto the scraggly beard. "Doctor says it's my heart. What do they call it, digestive or congestive something? If I drop dead tomorrow, there won't be one person who cares. Oh, Percy and Dave will use it as an excuse to drink a bottle of rum, but there's not one other person who would give a hoot. Not Henry or Margaret, not my grandchildren, and not Keefe, for sure.

"Now, I'm pretty tired. I never was one for talking much.

I do have my good days, but today ain't one. Nice to meet you, but I'm not up to any more socializing. Think you could find your way out?"

"Yes. I'll let you rest now, and I do appreciate your time. Mr. Rogers, I am writing this story, Keefe's story, and I make no apologies for that, but I want you to know I'm going to do my best to tell it truthfully."

"Well, no one could fault you for that. It's about time some truth was told."

Summer sat in the car for a few minutes before leaving Tom Rogers's yard. The interaction with Keefe's uncle had taken her by surprise. His words, the crackle in his voice, and the tears had been so unexpected. Summer wasn't sure just what she'd expected, but the emotion she saw in Tom Rogers was genuine. He was not a monster. He was a sad, lonely, broken man who had a side in this story.

"About time some truth was told," he'd said. That is what she would try to do. She was finally ready to begin. Summer Barkley would write a novel attempting to tell the real story leading up to the disaster that took the lives of her husband's parents and altered the course of Keefe William's life. She'd done the research, asked the questions, and now she needed to just sit at her keyboard and let the story unfold. Just as Keefe allowed the brushstrokes to create an image, she was ready to conjure up the words, to bring this long-hidden story to light.

PART THREE: THE STORY
1928

Helen Cronk traipsed into the kitchen decked out from head to toe as if she were attending a coronation, not walking two miles to get on board Gerry White's scow and head across the Saint John River to a church service at Beulah Camp.

"Missionaries from the bowels of Africa won't be impressed by your getup, but I don't figure it's the Sterritt sisters you hope to impress," Vera Cronk teased her sister while quickly changing her own footwear.

"Gerry said he was leaving at three o'clock sharp if any of us sorry arses wanted to be on board," Helen hollered as they headed out the door.

"How many of us sorry arses are going?"

"How would I know?" Helen replied. "I suppose if the Fullerton boys did up their chores in time they might sneak away. This morning's shower dampened the hay, so they won't need to get back to bring it in tonight. I think Tom Rogers is going, but more than that I don't know. I just know I am not going to miss today's gathering at the tabernacle."

"What you really don't want to miss is the gathering of Browns Flat boys. They're just the same as the ones on this side, you know, Helen."

Vera tried her best to keep up with her sister as they ran down the narrow path out onto the open beach and across the concrete slabs of the wharf to where the scow bobbed in the rippling water. She'd almost turned her ankle several times walking along the road wearing these stupid shoes. She quickly sat herself on a seat in Gerry's scow and slipped off her footwear.

The crossing was uneventful except for the one spot in the channel where Gerry nearly ran the scow aground. The water was low after the dry summer, which made the river bottom unpredictable.

God forbid, Vera thought, if a sudden pitch of the scow fetching up had knocked Miss High and Mighty into the drink. She leaned down to put her torturous footwear back on. Going barefoot would probably not be acceptable to the Reformed Baptists.

Vera had attended services at Beulah Campground before, although never without her parents. When she was younger the whole family would board the *DJ Purdy* and sail across the river at least once during the week of camp meetings in early July. Vera always clutched her mother's hand tightly, as the crowds entering the tabernacle were larger than any she'd seen before in one place.

No hand to clutch today; Helen had run ahead with the

group of boys and they were already partway up the hill. Perhaps the music Vera could hear was calling to them like the Pied Piper leading the rats from Hamlin.

Vera limped up the hill toward the hexagonal tabernacle. By the time she got to the open door it seemed too foreboding to enter. She wished Gladys had been allowed to come, but Gladys's father delivered quite a tirade when she'd asked his permission yesterday.

"No good comes from cavorting with those Baptists. You're an Anglican, and we don't mix with Bible pounders. 'Holier than thou' doesn't hold water with me. You get enough religion on Sunday; you don't need to go clear across the river for church on a Saturday afternoon."

Was it religion Vera was after by coming here today, or were her motivations as self-serving as her sister's? Vera searched the rows of benches for Helen and the others. The sawdust-covered floors seemed spongy and uneven. The last thing she wanted was to draw attention to herself by falling face first in the aisle. Prostrate before the Lord.

Vera quickly decided to squeeze onto the nearest bench instead of looking any longer for the crowd of Long Reachers she'd arrived with. The music livened up, and those around her stood up, breaking into song.

"Would you be free from the burden of sin?
There's power in the blood, power in the blood."

Vera did not recognize the song, but by the chorus she was singing and swaying along with the others. She was not, however, clapping her hands. She'd never seen a show of this kind at St. James. Sometimes Gertie Galbraith would speed the verse up a notch or two and hit a pitch all her own, but the rest of the congregation would continue the slow, steady chant Reverend Harding expected, barely looking up from their songbooks. Gertie's singing had sent her and Helen into fits of laughter one day, causing Father to decree they weren't to sit beside each other during Sunday service anymore.

"There is power, power, wonder-working power in the blood of the Lamb."

Vera was glad when the song ended and the crowd sat down. All the talk of blood was making her a bit queasy. Sometimes Father would make her hold the chicken on the block while he brought the axe down and cut its head off. Blood would spray up and one time she got some in her mouth. She'd run into the house crying and gagging. Mother had chastised her.

"Do you think your Aunt Alice got sick to her stomach over a little bit of blood? She wouldn't have made much of a nurse if she had, now would she?"

A tall man replacing the shorter one who'd been leading the singing stepped up to the raised podium and let out a booming "Amen." Choruses of "Amen!" and "Praise the Lord!" echoed through the building. When the chorus dissipated, Vera looked down the row to see people leafing through Bibles to find the scripture passage the man had instructed them to turn to.

Vera hadn't thought to bring a Bible. She certainly wouldn't have brought the big, red, leather family Bible that sat on the table in the parlour. She could have asked to borrow Aunt Alice's white nurse's Bible, but Mother would never have let her, knowing she would be crossing open water with it.

"Would you like to look on with me?" a voice asked, and for the first-time Vera realized that in her haste to sit down, she had seated herself beside a boy who seemed to be about her age. Helen would have no qualms about being so bold as to move closer and take the open Bible, but Vera's first urge was to jump up and relocate. But to ignore the invitation and leave pages of the opened Bible suspended seemed rude.

After a rousing service including more singing, a long message delivered by the preacher, and a moving account by the elderly Sterritt sisters of their last five years on the mission field, Vera was swept out of the tabernacle with the exiting crowd. The clump of people headed down the pathway toward a large building with a wide veranda on two sides. Entering a large hall, Vera deduced that as much as the Reformed Baptists enjoyed a time of rollicking music, booming scripture passages, and fiery pleas for salvation, they were just as passionate about their repast afterwards. Two long tables were covered with platters of turkey, beef, and ham, bowls of salads, plates of sandwiches, sweet breads, cookies, and fancy squares. Several pedestal plates held high, frothy cakes flanked by a variety of pies. Pots of tea and coffee and pitchers of lemonade were on a smaller table.

Vera searched the room for Helen, the Fullerton boys, or Tom Rogers. Surely they had attended the service and followed the people into this reception. Her search was fruitless, but as she turned her head she realized the boy she'd sat beside was right behind her. She hadn't looked up at his face during the service, but she recognized the grey flannel pants, argyle socks, and brown leather loafers. She looked to his white shirt and then allowed her gaze to take in the boy's handsome face and yellow curls. A tanned arm reached out to shake her hand.

"Hi. I'm Austin, and your name is?"

Vera took the boy's hand nervously. "I'm from across the river." Vera knew a certain reputation preceded her and regretted her feeble response. Hers wasn't the first generation of young folk to venture over the river to scope out the possibilities that a full Beulah Camp brought each summer. "I came to hear the Sterritt sisters," she added.

"From across the river or why you came doesn't tell me your name. I figured you hadn't been here all week or you'd probably know who I am. Being the preacher's son doesn't give me much anonymity."

"Vera. My name is Vera."

"Well, let's fill our plates, Vera, and hightail it out of here."

*

"Where the hell have you been?" Helen hollered as Vera

hopped breathlessly onto the scow. Her heart was thumping from the run down the hill, sure that the scow had left without her. She caught her breath before speaking.

"I could ask you the same thing."

"I didn't go to that stodgy church service, I'll tell you that. Turns out none of the boys had any intention of going either. I always heard the Beulah Camp boys were the cat's meow, but turns out it's the Browns Flat boys worth coming over for. And the Flat boys had liquor—not that I drank any, but the boys sure did. Here's hoping Gerry can row this scow, or it might be you and me rowing this damn thing."

*

In Vera's haste, she and Austin had only a quick goodbye, but Austin had shouted after her as she took off running down the hill, "There'll be a boat to bring folks over from your side for a baptism and picnic Friday afternoon. One o'clock. If you come, I'll be waiting for you."

For the next few days Vera didn't dare bring up the subject of returning to Beulah. It had been almost dark when she and Helen got back Saturday night, and Mother had herself in quite a state. Father was in bed when they came in but doled out a tongue lashing and a punishment the next morning, no doubt at his wife's urging.

"I'll not have my daughters out all hours of the night with such hooligans as Rexton Fullerton and Tom Rogers. Mother was frantic with worry. She was sure the river current had claimed you like it did the worshippers sailing with Captain Crawford on the fated June day in 1828."

"That was one hundred years ago, Father. These are modern times," Helen said, her voice a bit too animated, which did nothing to quell her father's anger.

"Watch your tongue, Helen. You are still under my roof. Do you really believe drowning in the river in 1928 will not leave you just as dead? And what if your poor mother had to bury both her daughters? I don't see any need of traipsing across the river chasing after boys. In my day, only loose girls were up to such a thing, and I'll not have my two daughters carrying on so."

Vera lifted the stove lid to drop two sticks in before moving the cast-iron frying pan onto the heat. She expected her father would keep delivering his lecture as long as his youngest daughter continued to make his morning coffee and prepare his breakfast.

"Wasn't just the wild girls crossing the river, was it, Dad?" Vera said quietly. "I'm sure I've heard Russell White tell the story of you, him, and a few others tipping an outhouse at Beulah one night and causing quite a stir."

"Good fun is all," Joe Cronk huffed. "Good clean fun, and not the consequences of being known as that kind of girl."

"What kind of girl is that, Father?" Vera asked.

"Enough lip from the two of you. No more trips across the river for the Cronk girls. There are plenty of church activities here on our own side."

Surprisingly, it was Marjorie Cronk who offered the opportunity for Vera to return to Beulah on Friday. Several of the ACW ladies were planning to go over, as a niece of Hilda Taylor's was being baptised.

"I am not giving up my Friday night to watch people in white robes get dunked in the river," Helen said. "There's a dance at the Clifton hall and I plan on going to that."

"I'd like to go, Mother," Vera said.

So, on Friday afternoon Vera was seated in the large Beulah Camp rowboat. The river was calm and the sun shone warmly down on the boatload of folks heading across for the annual event. Vera tried to quiet her excitement and nervousness by listening to the reminiscences of the others.

"I came over to my first baptism and picnic when I was just five years old," Hilda Taylor said. "Mother says I cried to be baptised. Father would have been horrified to think his daughter, who had already been properly baptised at the font at Trinity, wanted a Baptist river dunking. Mother's side was reformed Baptist, so Mother might have relented, but Father would have had none of it."

"I don't much care how the Baptists do it, but I've always enjoyed their picnics," Marjorie Cronk stated. "My sisters and I came over every summer. We figured it was a strong sermon at Beulah that persuaded Alice to follow a life of service."

"A life of poverty, you mean," Laura White added. "The pittance paid to nurses even in this modern day is criminal. And her without a husband to provide for her."

"Alice never cared much for fancy things. She was content to care for others and leave her sustenance to the Lord."

"Still think we should have brought something along for the picnic. Do they think Long Reach woman can't cook?" Doris Bradley said.

"I don't think they think that at all," Isabel Hamilton answered. "Pastor Mitchell's wife said the invitation to the Long Reach ACW came with no expectation of the ladies cooking or bringing anything. 'Just come enjoy a nice free afternoon,' she said, although I don't know who she thinks will be making our men's suppers tonight."

"Helen will make Joe's," Marjorie said.

Vera bristled at her mother's words. It hadn't been Helen who'd put the crock of beans in the oven. And who had gotten up early enough to set the rolls and bake them before getting ready to leave? Not Helen, for sure. It would be a small miracle if Helen even bothered to keep the wood fire going so the beans would cook for Father's supper. And would she bother doing up the dishes before rushing off to the Clifton hall? Likely the dishes would be waiting for Vera to do when she came home.

"Helen is growing up so fast, Marjorie. And she's a beauty," Doris said. "I bet the boys are beating your door down to court her."

Vera stifled a grunt. She dropped her hand to the side of the boat, letting her fingers glide in the cool water. Would Austin be waiting on the wharf? Would he remember his invitation, or had he by now completely forgotten the girl he'd met almost a week ago? The time they spent together had certainly been memorable for Vera. Austin Mitchell was such a gentleman, and so different from the boys she knew. He was funny and smart. He'd done most of the talking as they left the hall and wound their way down a narrow path passing cottages and onto the beach beside a small white chapel. He'd pulled a quilt off a clothesline at the last cottage on the path, spreading it on the sand before gesturing for her to sit down. "Have a seat, my lady, and let's enjoy our feast," he'd said in an exaggerated British accent.

Vera had giggled nervously. She'd been quite hungry but didn't want to wolf down the food as if she hadn't eaten in a week. She waited until Austin took the first bite before picking up a sandwich and daintily taking a nibble.

"What about you, Vera? Are the boys breaking down the door after you?" Hilda asked.

"I think that young Jud Williams has his eye on you," Isabel added.

"I don't think Vera has even started noticing boys yet," Marjorie Cronk said. "She's not my boy-crazy one."

Vera saw Austin as soon as the rowboat came in sight of the wharf. There were lots of people milling about on the wharf and more people walking the road leading up the hill, but Vera picked him out of the crowd with no trouble. He was waiting for her just as he said he would. Hopefully she could blend into the crowd and walk up the hill beside him without her mother noticing.

"There's a young people's service at the chapel by the river," Isabel Hamilton said. "You don't mind if Vera heads to that while we go to the service at the tabernacle, do you, Marjorie?"

"Not at all," Marjorie replied. "I don't worry about my Vera. She's got a good, sensible head on her shoulders. Just follow the other young people, Vera, and I'm sure you'll be able to find the chapel. I will see you at the baptism, dear."

Getting into bed later that night, Vera went over the day in her mind. There had indeed been a dishpan full of dirty dishes to do when she got home, and the kettle with no hot water in it. She'd gotten the fire going better, filled the kettle, and waited for it to heat before filling the dishpan. But any angry thoughts had been completely pushed out by her euphoria.

Austin had greeted her with enthusiasm, making her feel like he'd been anticipating her return. He presented himself as a gentleman and even asked if he could put his arm around her waist as they walked up the hill. Vera felt so important, so special, quickly registering the looks of a few of the girls they passed as she walked to the chapel with him. She could only imagine the stir it caused, a girl from across the river walking with the handsome son of the preacher.

"I'd love to keep you all to myself for the afternoon," Austin said. "But Father would notice right away if his own son was absent from the service. He even has me reading scripture this afternoon, but I told him I was expecting company and wouldn't help him with the baptism. I told Mother I would introduce you to her after the baptism. Maybe during the picnic we can sneak away and have some time alone."

The time alone had been brief but long enough to fuel the fire Vera felt building. The kiss had been very brief too, just a peck, barely hitting its mark, brushing her top lip, really—but a kiss nevertheless. Vera Cronk's first kiss was from the most handsome, most dashing and gentlemanly boy she had ever met. And their parting today had been a lingering clasp, a hug, a coming together. As Vera recalled it, her heart leaped in her chest.

"I'm only here for one more week," Austin said before Vera got on the boat, "and I hope I get to see you again. There will be a boat to pick up folks for the last service Sunday morning, and Father says a barge is going over on Saturday to pick up young folks for the rally on Caton's Island. A service on the beach there followed by a cookout is always held for the young people on the last Saturday of camp meeting. That's at least two times you'd have a way over, and I hope you can come both days. I'll be here all week if you catch any other way over."

A while later Helen slid into bed beside her and started chattering, even though Vera was pretending to be asleep.

"I never left the dance floor all night. Helen Cronk is no wallflower. I got passed from boy to boy and had them waiting in line. Tom Rogers has two left feet, though. And he kept butting in like he was my boyfriend or something. Speaking of boyfriends, Mother says you've caught the eye of the preacher's son. What's that all about?'"

Vera stayed silent, squeezing her eyes shut and resisting the urge to roll over and tell her sister about Austin. She knew better than to divulge anything to Helen. Helen always wanted anything she even suspected her sister laid claim to.

Vera breathed deeply, forcing a grunt-like snore, hoping her sister would shut up and go to sleep and leave her alone with the precious memories of her day still playing in her head. She'd had two lovely afternoons with Austin Mitchell, and she just wanted to think of how many times she could get across the river before he left.

*

"The phone is for you, Vera."

Vera grabbed the cloth off the roller on the back of the pantry door. She seldom got phone calls and had no time for them. If the bread was to rise in time to get it baked for dinner, she needed to get it into the pans.

"Hello?"

Vera could hardly make out what Gladys was saying. No doubt several other telephones had been picked up when the Cronks' ring came across. It rang so seldom, folks probably thought it an emergency of some kind.

"Father is going to Browns Flat this afternoon. He said we could come along. He's got some business to do with Mr. Baleman over there, which means we could be there a spell. You want to go, don't you?"

Vera had confided with Gladys and told her just how smitten she was with the young man she'd met at Beulah. She had also shared her hopes of seeing him at least one more time before a distance far greater than the width of the Saint John River separated them.

"Yes, of course I do, but what will I tell Mother?"

"Tell her I want the company. She knows Father would drag me along to row home just in case he has a few too many while trying to get a fair price for his yearlings. And I'll busy myself, Vera. I won't hang around with you and your beau."

Somehow she managed to convince her parents to allow her to go with Gladys, and it was Vera coming in late on Wednesday night.

Helen let out an angry grunt and pulled at the blankets. "Don't come in here all giddy and ridiculous. I had to make supper and clean up. Mother left right away for church group and Father made me feed those two deadbeats he had threshing his oats. Great night for you to be gone gallivanting across the river. Don't think you're going to that rally without me on Saturday. I'm not getting stuck doing all your work again."

Vera was not going to let Helen dampen her good mood. She and Gladys had had supper with Austin's family. They had treated Vera like a welcome guest and had been so interested when she mentioned her hopes of someday studying to be a nurse like her aunt and going to the places the Sterritt sisters had talked about. Vera couldn't believe she had spoken those words out loud.

Afterwards Gladys stayed behind to help with the dishes while Vera and Austin took a stroll alone down to the river. They talked about the future they could have if he became a doctor, her a nurse, and they travelled together to the mission field. Austin had not made her feel the least bit silly or naïve, but held her close, vowing it was fate that caused her to take a seat beside him in the tabernacle twelve days ago.

"Father says the Lord hears and answers our prayers, and I believe he sent you my way to show me his plan for my life. I know the months apart will be difficult, but I can devote myself to my studies knowing that when the year is over I will be right back here and you will just be a river crossing away. We will have two more times together before we will rely on letters in our months apart."

The kiss that followed was longer, more romantic, and hit its mark in every important way. Helen's grumbling was not going to take away the feeling Austin's lingering kiss had left.

*

Marjorie Cronk opened the door a crack, not wanting to wake her daughter. Days had passed and Vera hadn't dressed, hadn't eaten, and had only left the shaded darkness of her room for trips to the outhouse. The weeping had stopped, but the very life had drained from her. Marjorie would have to call Dr. Leatherbarrow if this deep funk did not lift soon.

The Mitchell boy's body had washed up on shore way upriver and was found today, but no one had breathed a word of it in Vera's presence. She'd been hysterical when they'd first had word he was missing. Apparently, he'd not been on the scow when it arrived at Caton's and everyone had just assumed he had stayed behind. After his parents and his two sisters returned and there was no sign of him, a search party was formed on land. Then after a cottager's rowboat was reported missing, the searchers took to the river.

"No one knows what would possess the boy to take a rowboat and head to Caton's on his own. He wasn't even a swimmer," Tick Smith said.

"Your girls were over to that rally, weren't they?" Tick asked.

"Helen was," Joe Cronk replied. "Vera missed the scow. Came back to the house in an awful state. Just as well she missed it, I think, considering what took place. Good Lord, she could have been in that rowboat with the young fella. Youngins have no sense."

1929

Vera stood outside and in the still night air could hear the music coming from across the river. Tears streamed down her cheeks. She thought the tears had dried up months ago, but the first night of camp meeting had been on her mind all day. She couldn't believe Helen had made such a big deal about going. The last few weeks she had put on quite a show, claiming she couldn't wait until Beulah time came around. She told them she had a life-changing conversion at Caton's Island.

"I asked the lord Jesus to be my saviour, but I didn't tell you at the time. What with the drowning and all, you didn't need me going on about it. Folks claim they saw a girl in the rowboat with the Mitchell boy, you know."

Helen had spoken those hateful words just a week ago and Vera had been completely speechless. How was it that now Helen knew this piece of information? She hadn't said anything about any of it in the weeks and months that followed Austin's death. How would Helen know such a thing? And if there had been a girl with Austin, what had become of her? No body had been found and no girl reported missing as far as Vera knew. What a heartless thing for Helen to tell her. She knew how devastated Vera had been with Austin's death. And how guilty she felt. If she hadn't been so stupid and missed the scow, Austin probably would have just got on it with her at the wharf, they'd have had their afternoon together, and…

"I don't suppose you want to come with me tonight?" Helen had asked her earlier.

Vera didn't look up, just continued peeling potatoes, determined not to show Helen any emotion.

"You have to get over it, Vera. You don't really think he'd have waited a whole year for you, do you? Stop your pining over a boy you barely knew. If you don't start going out and paying some attention to the boys right in your backyard, you'll be an old maid before you know it. I'm stepping out with Tom Rogers tonight. I just told him if he has any interest in winning me over he'd better be willing to come to camp meetings with me. Jesus first, I told him."

"Jesus," Vera muttered under her breath. Helen was so full of shit. It was Helen Cronk first and always would be.

1936

Jud Williams rose from the wooden bench at the back row of the auction ring and made his way to the cashier's window. He had not intended to buy a horse. Vera would accuse him of getting caught up in the auction's frenzy and completely taking leave of his senses. She was the keeper of the purse, of every hard-earned dollar and cent, and she had allowed him to take forty-five dollars to the sale only after considerable pleading on his part.

Some men might not stand for their wives to have such control, but Jud had no illusions regarding his shortcomings. He was a hard worker and could turn his hand at lots of things, but managing money was not one them. Without Vera's frugal ways they never could have saved the money to buy the forty acres from Stan Whelpley last year. Living with Vera's parents these last three years had helped them to do that, and she was now determined to save enough to start building in the spring. As far as Jud was concerned, he and Vera made a good pair, and he did not mind giving her the reins when it came to finances.

Jud had asked for money this morning without specifying what he wanted to purchase in Sussex. "I might stop into the auction. Ernie said last week the weanling pigs were going for a steal. I thought I might look for a new peevee and might see what Moffat's has in for winter galoshes. I can probably patch my old pair again, but I'll just see what the price of a new pair might be. We could use a few more laying hens. Sometimes you can pick up a few outside the auction house."

Even as he rambled on, he felt just how weak his arguments were. If he had come right out and said, "I'm looking to buy a horse," he knew Vera would not have parted with the money she'd taken from the jar and reluctantly given him before he left. He could have mounted some good arguments for a horse, but knowing Vera, she would counter each of his good reasons with a better one.

"Three years without a home to call our own is long enough," had been her strong retort a few months ago when he tried to convince her another year with her parents was the best plan. He knew just buying the property beside Helen and Tom was not enough to satisfy Vera. Shortly after Helen's wedding, five years ago, Tom had purchased a parcel of land with a decent house on it. But Jud knew the emotion he heard in his wife's voice whenever they discussed building was about more than the fact she didn't have a house to call her own.

For the most part Vera kept her emotions at bay and rarely let Jud see the vulnerability he knew was just below the surface. A deep sorrow, people called it. A lost love, a broken heart. He'd known all that when he'd started his pursuit of Vera, and he was fine being her second choice. Some men might have been swayed with Helen's flirty ways and not bothered to see that the real gem was Vera. Their love had been a slow blossom, but he had no regrets.

Helen was expecting her third child. Vera tried to hide her disappointment each month when after three years of marriage she had not found herself in the family way. It wasn't from lack of trying, and Jud kept reassuring Vera it would be her turn soon. Lately, Vera had taken the notion that if they built their own house she would get pregnant right away.

This horse was necessary for that undertaking—the house-building, not the impregnating, Jud thought, chuckling to himself as he walked to where his truck was parked. He would build a good lean-to and put the horse right on their property. He would use her to haul the logs he had already started cutting. He would clear a good-sized lot and get the logs to Waddell's mill and make the trade for the lumber he would need to build the house in the spring. He'd get to work digging a hole for the basement as soon as the ground thawed. He would haul the rocks from the several piles along the property line and build a good solid foundation. This horse would prove her worth. These were the arguments he would arm himself with when he returned with the five-year-old Percheron and nothing he'd mentioned earlier or anything on Vera's list. Hopefully she would see his purchase had been a sound one, even if it had taken every dollar she had allowed him to bring with him to Sussex.

*

Vera stepped down off the rickety ladder. Helen had refused to help with papering the sitting room. She could understand her sister being timid to climb this pathetic stepladder Father had cobbled together with wire instead of breaking down and buying a new one, but Helen could have kept her feet safely on the floor and at least passed her the strips of wallpaper. But no, Mother and Helen had been sitting comfortably in the kitchen for the last hour, sipping their afternoon tea while she struggled with this damn wallpaper as well as tending to Helen's three-year-old, who was trying his best to knock over the bucket of wallpaper paste.

"Jud just drove in, Vera," Helen called from the kitchen. "Looks like he might have bought something, and it's not a cow's head I see. It's a horse, I think."

"I just have two more strips left to hang. I'm not quitting until I get it done. Come get Henry before he upends this ladder with me on it. Take him out to see whatever godforsaken creature Jud saw the need to buy. I knew better than to let him take that much money to Sussex on a sale day. Just what we don't need, a horse. Surely he knows hay costs money."

"Oh, don't be such a grump. How you got Jud Williams with your nasty disposition is beyond me, Vera. A man will only take so much of a wife nagging the life out of him."

"Helen, come pass that last strip up to me and mind your own business."

*

"Her name is Dolly, but we can change it if you like."

"Can we change the price you paid for her or the cost of oats and the hay it will take to feed her through the winter? And where do you propose you're going to put her? Father has little enough room in the barn for the animals he's got, and she looks like she'll need a lot of head room."

"She's a good size, all right. Seventeen hands high. She's had one foal already. We'll get her bred next year and sell her foal to get some of our money back. By then, maybe we'll have a decent barn built. For now, I'm going to put up a good lean-to with room for her and the hay we'll need for the winter. By spring I'll have a bit of pasture fenced for her. It's not too late to seed the field nearest the river."

"Oh, you've got it all figured out, don't you? A lean-to can't be built for nothing, you know. And after the dry summer we've had I'm sure buying hay isn't going to be cheap. Father got what he figured he needed right out from the field and the price was higher than what George charged last year. It being late October will give them more reason to hike the price up. You don't get nothing cheap from Fullerton's. Can't blame them, though; they're the ones putting the labour into it.

"And even if you've got enough logs cut for a lean-to, Lorne Waddell isn't going to mill them for nothing. And where are you going to get all this extra time to build a decent shelter before the snow flies? And what about getting there morning and night to feed her when you're working? And the creek will freeze up soon, then how are you going to get water to her?"

"The well on the place is still good, Vera. I'm going to put a well house over it and insulate it good. If I keep the ice off it, I should be able to draw from it all winter. I was thinking I'd put a big enough lean-to up so on the nights before I plan to go lumbering, I'll camp right out there."

"Don't expect me to camp there with you. I don't plan on moving there until I have a decent and comfortable house to live in."

"By this time next year you will, Vera. I'm going to work every spare minute I have in order to get the wood cut, and by spring we'll be ready to start building. This beautiful girl will haul out my logs right to the road, and I won't have to count on anyone else. I'll have a good-sized load to get hauled to the mill before the roads close in March."

"Well, I guess we've got her, don't we? You'll have to put her in the paddock here for now. I best get in and start supper. You can be sure Helen in her delicate state wouldn't think of putting her hand to getting a meal ready. She'll be more than happy to stay and eat it, though. And Mother, for some reason, considers me the chief cook around here as part of our room and board. The chief everything, it seems. You can't get a house built on our place fast enough for my liking. Now don't go getting yourself knocked out getting that horse off the truck by yourself. She's liable to be spooked after her trip from Sussex. Here comes Tom up the lane. Wait and get him to help you."

Making her way back to the house, Vera reflected on her day. She had not intended to greet Jud in the manner she had. She'd been so anxious to see him when Helen announced his arrival, but as usual her true feelings were masked with the nasty, judgemental tone she always presented. She couldn't even imagine what everyone would think if she said out loud the things she really felt. When taking Margaret from her mother's arms this morning, the flood of emotion almost disarmed her. Seeing Helen with two precious little ones and pregnant again so soon was a heartbreak she carefully covered up.

"This child reeks. Can nobody else smell the load she has in her diaper? Dear God. Would anything get done around here if I didn't do it?" Vera had mumbled under her breath.

"Would you be a dear and change the baby, Vera? You can't imagine how nauseous I have been feeling and changing her diapers just about does me in," Helen had said.

I shouldn't be taking it out on Jud, Vera thought. *God knows he tries his best. God love him. He had no idea what he was getting himself into, marrying Vera Cronk. It seems as soon as the ink dried on our wedding certificate I turned into an old shrew. Three years under his in-laws' roof has not helped. Who could blame him if he decides to take up residence in a lean-to with a horse?*

I'll make him an upside-down apple cake for his supper. Maybe dessert will make up for the welcome I just gave him.

*

The Percheron mare allowed herself to be backed down the makeshift ramp and then walked calmly through the gate into the paddock.

"She's a beaut, Jud," Tom said. "Train her right and she'll be great in the woods. My father always said, the best tool a man can take to the woods is a strong horse. A horse can go where a tractor can't. And you've got some steep hills on your place."

"We both have some steep hills, but lots of good-sized trees. I had Stan in to look and he thinks I should get enough logs just off the section beside the brook to build a good-sized house. Vera wants a two-storey like the Holders'. I'm getting Bill Henderson to draw up the plans for me. I haven't told Vera yet. He's going to draw up a whole set showing the house from all sides and the floor plan for both storeys."

"Helen says Vera's been out of sorts lately. Having a new house to look forward to should cheer her up a bit. Talking about being out of sorts, Helen's been no ray of sunshine herself. She's sick as a dog every morning. She was with the other two but it passed before this. Here's hoping she feels better real soon."

1937

Vera turned the knob on the RCA Victor until the static settled and the sound was clear. She turned up the volume.

"It's coming on now, Mother. Charlie McCarthy's not a person, Father. He's a dummy. Edgar Bergen is a ventriloquist. A ventriloquist, Father. You know, he speaks for the puppet without making his lips move."

"He's on the radio, for goodness' sake, Vera. How can you tell he doesn't make his lips move?"

"Just listen, Father. It's coming on. Sit closer if you can't hear it."

"Where's Jud?" Joe Cronk asked. "Isn't he coming in for the show?"

"He's just getting back from feeding Dolly. He'll be right in. Now stop talking."

"But I thought I saw Bill Henderson drive up."

"Quiet, Joe. We're going to miss the whole show if you keep talking."

"Fine. Let a wooden box rule our lives. What did we ever do before radio?"

*

Jud got out of his truck and walked across the yard to greet Bill Henderson.

"Only someone as handy as you could keep such an old beast running," said Bill. "You've replaced most of the parts on the truck, haven't ya', making one wonder if it can still be considered a 1924 Chevrolet."

"Have you got those plans drawn up, Bill?"

"Yeah, hope I'm not interrupting anything. My boys were all lined up on the parlour rug listening to 'The Lone Ranger.' I got sent out for making too much noise. I don't know what Mavis was thinking, bringing Marconi's invention into the house. It's hard enough to get those boys out in the wintertime to do their chores, but now they plan everything around those confounded radio dramas. And Mavis won't miss her story when it comes on."

"Vera listens to 'The Guiding Light' too. She usually sneaks down the road to visit Gladys when it's on so they can listen to it without interruption. With Weldon away working in the States, Gladys has more free time than the rest, or so Vera says."

"Oh I know, I hear the same thing. I would think Gladys with five little ones would be just as busy as the others, but according to what I hear, it's us men running these women ragged."

"It seems it's just one big party at Gladys's, and I'm sure Vera just tells me the half of it. Why, they had bonfires all summer, and from what I gather wearing bathing suits was optional. At least they waited until after dark, or the crew on the *Majesta* would have tipped the riverboat over getting a look at our woman."

"Even a look is more than I get these days, I can tell you. Mavis has been so busy with the new one. He's colicky and barely sleeps ten minutes in a row. About these plans, did you tell Vera you were getting me to draw them?"

"No, I've been keeping it as a surprise. It hasn't been easy, since all she talks about is the house. She wants it to be as grand as the Holder place. Were you able to work in a wide veranda on the front, facing the river?"

"Well, let's take them in and lay them out on the kitchen table and I'll show you what I came up with."

Vera's hearty laughter greeted the two men as they walked into the kitchen.

"She won't be too happy about me interrupting her show, but once she sees what you've brought, she might feel differently about being torn away from Charlie McCarthy's antics."

"Now, when did you ask Bill to do these up?" Vera asked once she stopped grumbling and had a good long look at the top sheet on the stack of papers on the kitchen table.

"He came down a couple of months ago and asked me to see what I could do with the ideas you have for the house," Bill replied.

"And here I thought all the talking I was doing was going in one ear and out the other. I wouldn't blame Jud for blocking my rantings and ravings out. I suppose some things I want aren't even possible. I must think I'm a Crosby or an Oland with my big ideas. A simple two storey with no fancy features is more than I can even hope for with the way things seem to be this winter. Jud works night and day and it's very mean spirited of me to want more than we can afford. The picture you've drawn looks real nice, Bill."

"I've told Bill everything you've been talking about. He's done up the floor plans, Vera. Haven't seen them myself yet, but I do see he's given you the front veranda you've been dreaming of."

"The veranda in the front faces the river. There's a little veranda on the back too," Bill added.

"He has the house nestled into the hill, which gives us the flatter land for our pastures and outbuildings. It puts us a distance from the river, which will shelter us a bit from those cold winds whipping across in the winter."

"We'll be right up against Helen and Tom's line. Make sure you get the survey stakes right or Helen will be laying claim to my pantry or something," Vera said.

"You're too hard on your sister," Jud replied.

"Oh, really. She and Tom are both as tight as a crab's ass and as waterproof. If they thought we built one inch over onto their property, they'd be asking for rent. And God forbid you cut one tree on Tom's property. He's got them counted, I think."

"Look at the floor plans Bill's done up, Vera. You've got a dining room and a good-sized parlour."

Vera took the second-floor plans off the table. She fought back tears as she gazed at the three good-sized bedrooms Bill had fit in the T-shaped upper floor separated by a main hall. Three bedrooms to fill with the children they were expected to have. *If only expectations were enough,* thought Vera. A house full of children. A quiver full. A family to carry on the Williams name. All these expectations had been voiced over and over by family, friends, and perfect strangers in the years since she and Jud had walked down the aisle at St. James. Several people had believed Vera Cronk must have already been in the family way to have snared the handsome Jud Williams.

Each month as Vera waited for her menses, she hoped those expectations would finally come to be. But each month the red flow would greet her and once more quash those expectations and the dream Vera had held in her heart for as long as she could remember. This house would be built, she had no doubt. Jud was a hard worker and a good provider. He was always so generous and so willing to give her the desires of her heart. He would fill those bedrooms if it were up to him. But perhaps it was her preventing the dream from coming true.

*

Vera looked out the window at the truck in the Cronks' dooryard. Hamie Nichols was heading into Saint John today and she had her Eaton's order ready for him to take in. The two dollars she was sending along with it seemed extravagant, but she had her heart set on the items she had chosen from the catalogue. If she bought a few things every few months, she would be all set when they moved into the house, hopefully by Christmas or before the heralding in of 1938.

Vera had been down to the property yesterday and was impressed with the number of logs Jud already had piled at the road. She'd waited for him to come back across from Grassy Island. Stan Whelpley declared there was eight inches of ice on the river, and that was enough to convince Jud to take the truck across for a load of hay. Vera hadn't even grumbled or tried to talk Jud out of buying it. Dolly was proving her worth.

"I'm going into town today, Vera, 'cause I'm thinking it's going to freeze up soon and then the ferry won't be running. Ozzie Saunders crossed the ice at the point yesterday with a load of beef."

"Lot of good a load of beef would do anyone at the bottom of the Kennebecasis River," Vera replied. "Jud crossed over to Grassy yesterday, but you wouldn't catch me crossing at the point just yet."

"Well I'll take my chances with the ferry today. The Pitts try to keep it running as long as they can. We had a cold January, but who knows, the thaw might come any day. We could be fighting mud on these roads soon enough. Is there anything else you or your mother want while I'm in the city?"

"We're good. Stan Edwards was by with the bread truck two days ago, and what you can't buy from him isn't worth wanting. But would you mind stopping in and checking with Helen? I know she was looking the catalogue over real close yesterday, and she probably made up an order."

"She's got another layette to prepare, don't she? What about you, any booties or little nighties in your Eaton's order, Vera?"

Vera turned away from Hamie and lifted the cook-stove lid. "Grab me a couple of sticks from the wood box, would you please? Do you care for a cup of tea before you head out? Father should be in from milking soon and would love to sit and wag the tongue with you."

"No, I better get going. Feels like snow in the air and I want to get back home before dark."

*

True to Hamie's prediction, the Gondola Point ferry stopped running the third week of February, and it looked like a long, frigid winter was in store. Jud fought a couple of snowstorms during the month but hitched Dolly up most every day to bring out at least a log or two. The plan was he would go to Long Island in March, helping to finish up the lumbering there before spring. Vera's hope of being pregnant before he packed up to go was shattered when she woke up on the last day of February in a pool of blood. She didn't even tell Jud but balled up all the bedclothes and shoved them into a feed bag, hiding it in the basement. She would burn them later. Very wasteful, she knew, but scrubbing them in the washtub would only bring attention to her troubles.

Mother had stopped asking every month, but Vera wished she could say the same for every busybody on the Reach. Yesterday at Nagle's store her fertility or lack of it was the topic of conversation among the several people crowded into the small space. Even old Cal Smith said his piece from his perch on the nail keg. What does an old bachelor know or care about childbearing? What did anybody really know?

There were lots of women around who people figured had already been with child on the day of their nuptials. Some women got pregnant weeks after getting married and had babies every year until their change of life. Why was it some women had years between children? Her own mother had had her and Helen a year apart quite a while after getting married, and then there had been no more babies. Her mother said there were things a woman could do to keep from getting pregnant. But even nursing two sets of twins hadn't kept Mrs. Lamb from birthing six children in five years. And then there was Mrs. Hamilton next door with neither chick nor child, although the gossip claimed the same couldn't be said of her husband, Harold.

What did anyone know? Not even Dr. Leatherbarrow could tell Vera why she hadn't become pregnant yet. Last month when he'd come to treat Mother's quinsy Vera had asked him if there was any medicine she could take. His response was just telling her to make sure she was allowing regular relations. He said sometimes a woman doesn't want relations as often as the man but if she wanted to conceive she should make herself available every day when she wasn't menstruating.

Vera had barely made it to her room before bursting into tears after the delivery of Dr. Leatherbarrow's glib advice. She'd laid on her bed sobbing and finally fell asleep. It was dark when her mother had come to remind her supper needed getting. She did make herself available. Even nights when she was so tired she could hardly drag herself to bed and nights when Jud came in late after a day of hard work she always consented, sometimes even pleading with Jud to stay awake long enough to do the act. Lack of trying was not the problem, so apparently, a country doctor with experience setting broken bones, lancing boils, and delivering babies had very little to offer to a woman who appeared to be barren.

*

March was a dreary and drab month, and with the added work of caring for Henry and Margaret, Vera felt a heaviness she could barely mask. Helen had been put on bed rest and it was just assumed Vera would take over the children's care and keep them here with her. Jud was on the island, after all, and with Vera having no little ones of her own, who better than her to be the one to step up and help Helen?

Henry and Margaret were delightful children and it certainly wasn't their fault Vera was so full of anger and resentment. Henry was a busy little boy and Mother and Father could certainly not be expected to keep up with an active three-year-old. Mother would rock Margaret to sleep at naptime, but most of her care fell to Vera as well. What was a bit of extra laundry, two more mouths to feed, or the occasional sleepless night? Vera was young and poor Helen so weary and delicate in her last weeks of pregnancy.

Vera felt if she heard one more person say "Poor, dear

Helen," she would scream. How about poor, dear Vera? Does nobody think for one minute she might be weary, she might be exhausted, she might be fed up to her chin with the way everyone took her for granted? She hadn't heard anyone say "Poor, childless Vera" yet, but it would come soon enough. How much time would they give her and Jud? They were not newlyweds anymore, so how many years of grace would they be given?

Alice Carvell had not said as much yesterday when she dropped in with a quilt for Marjorie Cronk to put on, but what she had said gave Vera the impression her status was inching toward the branding of childless.

"You are a dear, Vera. Your sister is so fortunate to have you. Her little ones are precious, aren't they, and her with another blessing on the way. And isn't it a blessing of sorts you haven't any of your own yet? It would be a good bit harder to care for your sister's little ones if you had a brood of your own. But God hasn't seen fit to bless your home yet. It's not our place to question his wisdom, though, is it?"

Vera had poured tea into Alice's cup and quelled the urge to scald her neighbour's lap. Vera was sure the syrupy-sweet words were just the crust of the deep-dish pie of Alice's real thoughts on the subject of Jud and Vera Williams's childless marriage.

"Don't suppose you'll have much time to help your mother with my Churn Dash. You are such a beautiful quilter, Vera. Maybe when your mother has the bee next week you can find a little time to sit with the ladies. Those children nap, don't they? You'll be quilting a crib quilt real soon I'm sure, dear."

Having just put the children to bed, Vera was walking into the parlour when the "Fibber McGee and Molly" show was interrupted by a news bulletin.

"Listen, Joe," Marjorie Cronk called loudly across the room. "There's been an explosion."

"A what?" Joe Cronk said.

Vera sat down on the settee and turned up the volume.

"An explosion at a school, I think. Dear God," Marjorie answered.

"Where?" Joe asked.

"New London, Texas, Father."

"England?" Joe hollered.

"No, Texas, Father. I can't hear with you hollering questions. Let me listen."

The details of the massive gas explosion were too ghastly to believe. Sometime in the afternoon an explosion at the London School in New London, Texas, had lifted the roof off the building. The newscast said possibly over four hundred people, mostly children, had likely been killed. Rescuers were pouring in from all over the state.

Vera sat with her face in her hands. The tragedy's magnitude was more than she could grasp. Children caught in a fiery explosion. She began sobbing and shaking.

"What is wrong with Vera?" Joe shouted from across the room. "Turn off the damn radio, Marjorie. I told you no good would come from bringing that thing into the parlour. What was wrong with getting the news from Jim Bradley when he brings the *Kings County Record*?"

The terrible aftermath in Texas was on the minds and lips of everyone for the next week or so until a near tragedy closer to home took their attention. Mavis Henderson brought the news to the Cronk house. The youngest Johnston boy had been scalded. Bill had gone to Hampton early this morning to fetch Dr. Leatherbarrow. Apparently, the toddler had grabbed the kettle from off the stove and the boiling water had spilled out onto his tiny body. Poor Alice Johnston was in a terrible state. The child would live, but he had been burned pretty badly.

Vera went about getting the noon meal ready while Mavis sat telling Marjorie all she knew about the Johnstons' misfortune.

"I know Henry moves fast and you can't be up to what he'll do," Marjorie stated. "Poor Alice can't go blaming herself. Accidents happen. I always keep the kettle well back on the stove but it's so easy to be careless. God love the wee one. Speaking of Henry, where is he, Vera? Helen would not be able to bear it if something were to happen to her precious children."

Vera looked over to where Henry was sitting on the floor in the dining-room doorway, lining up a row of miniature tin cars. Margaret was close by, playing with the button bottle. Both pastimes were always good for a few minutes of distraction.

The cars had been Jud's. A fine collection they were, and every time Vera took the box out to let Henry play with the small metal vehicles, she would feel a twinge of longing, hoping the cars would someday be treasured by the sons she and Jud would have.

Precious children, Vera thought. What about the precious children of New London, Texas? At least 290 children had perished, they were saying; 290 treasured children someone had waited for and lived for, had dreams and hopes for; 290 children just gone in a fiery inferno in the blink of an eye. Little children pulled kettles down upon themselves, fell in the river and drowned like the little Gorham girl, swallowed what seemed like a harmless soldier bean and died of suffocation. Precious children perished and precious children were sometimes never born.

Vera found her thoughts were again spiralling to the melancholy and morbid. She would have to shake this gloomy thinking. Jud would be home soon and spring was in the air. Maybe spring would bring the desire of her heart. They would break ground and start the home Bill had drawn the plans up for. Perhaps by the time Jud carried her over the threshold she would be expecting her own precious child. Thoughts of accidents and mishaps were foreboding and the loss of a child tragic, but for every parent who welcomes a baby, the hope and happiness somehow overshadows the fear.

"I'm going to run over to see Alice Johnston when the

children go down for their nap after dinner," Vera said. "She must be beside herself. I'll pick Earle up a bag of penny candy at Nagle's on my way. It must have been frightening for the poor gaffer to see his little brother burned."

"Earle is nearly grown, you know. He's twelve I think," Mavis said. "Poor Alice lost several babies between him and the little one. Her little girl lived only a few hours. God love her. Seemed like there would be no more and then little Raymond was born."

"Why did she have so much trouble?" Vera asked.

"God knows," answered Mavis. "It's in his hands, you know. Each child is a miracle and a healthy baby is a gift."

Vera whisked Margaret up off the floor. The toddler's facial expression showed there would soon be a need to attend to her diaper. "Well, I'm sure the boy still likes penny candy," Vera said as she left the room with Margaret.

*

April 21, which happened to be Princess Elizabeth's eleventh birthday, was also the birthday of Helen's infant daughter, and she was subsequently given the name Elizabeth Evelyn Rogers. Vera saw the irony in the fact this newest baby would carry a royal moniker, as the infant's mother certainly regarded herself a queen. Not only was Vera expected to care for Henry and Margaret as well as prepare all the meals for two households for the next two weeks, she was attending to all the needs of this tiny infant, except of course for the feeding. The small mouth would find no sustenance at her breast. At the very least Helen had to trouble herself to feed her newborn.

*

Vera stared out the kitchen window toward the river. The ice was just about gone and the channel was free. Two weeks ago, the *Majesta* had been held up for hours at The Mistake until the ice floes passed. The snow was just about gone too and the roads were too muddy for cars to pass. Not even the mail would come today, as Jim Bradley had not ventured down the muddy roads all week. Two days ago, Vera had come back home and now just walked down a couple of times a day to Helen and Tom's. She still had the two older children with her, of course. With the children napping, she headed down to the lot with a lunch for Jud, who had started digging the hole for the foundation.

"This lunch was wonderful, Vera. I had planned on working until dark with just breakfast to hold me, so you were a welcome sight."

"I would hope you were happy to see more than just Mother's red picnic basket."

"Of course I was," Jud said, leaning over and giving his wife a lingering kiss.

"Don't get frisky, Jud Williams. You're not having your way with me in a lean-to or on the cold, wet ground. You need to put a house up before we fool around on this property."

"Oh now, Vera. Don't rule out our options. Once the weather warms up I thought we might pitch a tent and spend some nights on our own property."

"We'll see. Right now, until my sister gets her feet under her I have no free time to gallivant down here and fornicate with you."

"I know you are run ragged. It was real nice of you to bring me a picnic. I don't suppose Tom said anything about coming down to help me. As I recall I helped him put his new roof on when they moved into their house, and I helped him build his barn last year."

"Oh, they take the help for sure, but neither one trouble themselves with helping anyone else out. And God forbid I should say a word to criticize them. Mother chastised me this morning, accusing me of being hateful and self-centred. This is after two months of looking after the children and catering to Helen's every need. Tom could have hired someone. They have enough money, but no, they have an indentured servant at their beck and call."

"Don't let it get to you, Vera. You are twice the woman your sister is. Someday you will get your reward."

"When I'm dead, maybe."

"When we start building, you will just have to tell Helen you're too busy to look after the children. We'll set up a little cookhouse and move right down here for the summer. It will be a vacation for you."

"Yeah right, a vacation, cooking over a campfire like the

Maliseet women who set up camp on the shore all summer. Maybe I'll make baskets and sell them too."

"Camping out here will be great fun, Vera, and we'll be on our own place."

"I'll think about it. I'll let you get back to your digging. Maybe by July I'll move down here. I'll potty train Margaret first, since as God knows her mother won't get around to doing it. Why would she, when I wash all the diapers? Enough of my bellyaching. You'll be happy to see the back of me so you can dig in peace and quiet." She paused, then added sarcastically, "Until Tom comes to help you."

*

Joe Di Maggio hitting three consecutive home runs in a game against the St. Louis Browns was all the talk as Vera entered Nagle's store on the morning of June 14. She passed her long list to Mrs. Nagle.

"I'll get your order done up, Vera. All this baseball talk seems to have put a hold on work around here. These old codgers have been here for more than an hour. Apparently farming on the Reach has come to a standstill while we worship at the feet of a New York Yankee."

"We're finally moving down the road, Ella. Jud has the foundation in and he's ready to start framing the house up. I'm going to stay right there with him. He needs three good meals a day if he's going to keep up the pace. Besides, I can swing a hammer as good as any man."

"As good as any of these men, I can tell you; today, anyway, when they think swinging a bat at a stupid ball is the be all, end all. If we didn't keep things going, what would the men do? Helen has her strength back, does she?"

"She will manage. Her new baby is an angel and Henry just turned four. Margaret is toilet trained and isn't the care she was. Helen will be fine."

"It's time you looked out for your own affairs anyway, Vera. You've been a dear to help your sister and I hope she knows it."

"Well, that's another topic and not one I care to get into. I gave her lots of notice. She is right next door, but I don't expect she'll be over much and I'm not going there for a while. Mother can manage too, so right now my job is to look after Jud. He never complains, but he's gotten the short straw lately."

"I'm going to throw in some of the canned soups we just got in. Might come in handy for a quick meal, though it won't taste as good as what you'd make for sure."

"Thanks, Ella. Stop down sometime and see how the building's coming along. I feel like a newlywed finally setting up housekeeping for myself, even if it is in a tent and a cooking shelter." Vera set the supplies in the truck, then headed down the road. She was excited and anxious about this move. Of course, there would be some challenges camping out on the property, but she was more than ready for the adventure. And she had missed her time of month twice in a row. She hadn't mentioned it to Jud, but he would figure it out sooner or later. Perhaps preparing for this move was aligning the fates to finally grant the desire of her heart.

Vera turned off the road and onto the long, winding driveway. The house Jud was working so hard to build would be a home after all, and Vera would stay right here until the secret she was holding on to so dearly became evident.

Two weeks later, after three straight days of heavy rain, Vera was questioning her intention to stay on the property. Jud had moved their tent under the lean-to so at least the so-called bed they came to at night was dry. Jud had gone right to sleep as soon as he had laid his head down. The rain had not kept him from putting long days into the construction and he was now building the walls for the rooms on the second storey.

Vera had tried to help today, but she had not felt right since midafternoon. The first bit of cramping had been mild, the feeling that often-preceded menstruation. But her breasts were so tender and she was convinced this time she was really pregnant. Perhaps the slight cramping was typical of her condition. If it continued she would ask Gladys, maybe even tell her what she hoped.

By suppertime the cramping had become more severe and even in the dimness of candlelight Vera could see some spotting. Now as she lay here silently listening to Jud's snoring, the pain was almost more than she could bear.

Vera slid out of the sleeping bag and stood against the post. There was a sudden gush and a cramp caused her to cry out. Jud stirred but did not wake. Vera knew whatever was happening she would not be able to simply crawl back in beside Jud and quietly let it pass. She called out her husband's name.

*

The last few hours were a jumble in Jud's mind. Vera's sharp, piercing cry woke him from the deep sleep he had fallen into after a long and exhausting day. He'd groggily lit the lantern and was shocked to see a dark pool of blood at his wife's feet. He dressed quickly and picked Vera up in his arms, carrying her to the truck in the pouring rain. On the drive to her parents' house her cries did not subside. Amid her cries of pain, she pleaded with God not to take the baby.

Jud had begun in the last few days to wonder if Vera might be pregnant. The weeks since moving to the property had gone by quickly, and when he considered just how long they had been there he realized that Vera had not had a bleeding since they moved into the tent. They had worked long days side by side and most nights had lain together before sleeping. There had been no interruptions in their coupling. Upon that reflection he had decided to wait a while longer before asking her. He knew her sorrow if she had to tell him he was wrong.

And now as he carried her into her mother's spare room and laid her in bed, he feared that not only her pregnancy was ending but her life might be taken from him as well.

*

Jud paced the floor, waiting for Dr. Leatherbarrow to come out from the Cronks' spare room. The last hour had been a mix of cursing, praying, and begging. His first concern was for Vera's life. Nothing mattered as much as her survival. Vera would be heartbroken, but they would get through it. But he could not imagine losing her. His prayers and his pleas were for Vera's life, but his curses were for the baby, a child, the start of a family that God seemed unwilling to allow them.

"She's had a miscarriage," Dr. Leatherbarrow said as he approached Jud.

"She's not going to die, is she, Doc?"

"She will be all right, but she'll need some rest. I'm going to do a procedure in the morning to make sure everything is out. Do you know how far along she was?"

"She hadn't told me she was pregnant. This is going to kill her."

"Vera will be fine. She's young and fit as a fiddle. She'll be disappointed for sure, but it's for the best. These things happen for a reason. She can try again, but I'd say wait a few months. She needs to get her strength back. She should probably stay with her parents for a bit and I'd put a hold on relations for at least four weeks. She's sleeping now. I'll be back in the morning. You go try to get some sleep yourself, Jud. There's not a thing you can do for her right now."

1944

The snow was swirling and piling up quickly, the front steps almost covered. In the early-morning light Vera could see Jud making his way back from the barn to the carriage shed. He would hitch Dolly up to the sleigh and take the cream cans to the road before he came in for his breakfast.

Vera set the kettle full onto the heat. She'd have the coffee ready when Jud came in. If it were a weekday, Vera would be catching the cream truck to Summerville. She had started working for the Kingston Peninsula Telephone Company in October. Mother had a lot to say, being very critical of her daughter working outside the home, but Helen had defended her decision, albeit in her usual backhanded way.

"Mother, Vera has nothing to fill her days. She keeps a perfect home and always has her pantry full. With no little ones to chase after, she needs a little job to do."

A little job. Vera would like to see Helen work all day and then come home and put a meal on the table. Margaret at nine years old did most of the cooking and housework. Helen spent hours blackening her new Elmira cook stove and was perfectly happy to leave the rest to her young daughter. And Henry worked like a grown man at his father's side. Jud had tried to get Henry to work for him a few times, but Tom could never spare him.

The small salary Vera was now making was certainly helping to run the household. Prices were so high and work so scarce for Jud. He and Tom had been spared from being called up to serve, but being in a community filled with farmers, any extra work was quickly taken. Jud had three steers and four pigs slaughtered just before Christmas, which had helped. Vera carefully budgeted, so even with the high cost of everything they were managing.

Rationing made getting coffee and tea next to impossible. The coffee canister held only enough grinds for a couple more pots. Vera was making it much weaker these days than what Jud liked, but weak coffee was better than no coffee.

Vera enjoyed her job as operator. Being on the central switchboard was never boring and her days flew by. She took great pride in managing the constant task of receiving and sending calls. She also took the responsibility of protecting the privacy of callers very seriously. She had overheard many conversations, giving her more information about the peninsula residents than she cared to know, but she was not about to divulge anything she overheard.

"You must know where Malcolm MacDougall has gotten to," Helen had said yesterday. "Did he get any suspicious calls in the days before he went missing?"

Vera had heard nothing, but even if she had heard something, she would not have told her sister. She would have shared it with Malcolm's poor mother, who must be beside herself with worry.

It was the talk up and down the Reach how Malcolm MacDougall had gone out to the barn four days ago and not returned to the house. His brother and mother had heard no vehicles and there had been no tracks on the road. Malcolm MacDougall had disappeared as if into thin air.

Vera looked out the window again and could see Jud and Dolly stopped at the barn door. She broke two eggs into the frying pan.

*

Gladys tried not to laugh as she steadied her hand, guiding the eyebrow pencil up the back of Vera's leg while Vera tried to lie perfectly still, face down on her bed.

"We're being silly, Gladys. No one is going to believe we're wearing silk stockings. No one has could get their hands on a pair for months. Even Tom couldn't get Helen a pair, even though she believes their money will get them whatever her heart desires. She sees rationing as a personal attack."

"Well, whether they think it or not, you and I are going to strut proudly into the Pearl Hall tonight with our long legs looking beautiful."

"It seems almost unpatriotic to go dancing tonight so soon after D-Day."

"I know, but really we need to have some fun, Vera."

"I hate to even turn the radio on these days. Will this ghastly war ever end? I know it's worse for you with Weldon over there. I don't know how you stand it."

"Let's just do our best to enjoy ourselves tonight. Now, do *my* legs before Jud comes upstairs to see what's keeping us."

When Gladys and Vera entered the kitchen a half an hour later, Jud was sitting at the kitchen table, not appearing anxious to leave or to have been waiting for them at all.

"He makes my blood boil," Jud said when he looked up.

"What has he done this time?" Vera asked, not even having to inquire who had upset Jud so badly.

"Tom's hired Dave Evans to lumber his place next winter. He knows I would have put a crew in there. It would be so close for me. If I don't get the Holder place, I'll be clear over in Whitehead all winter. He didn't even give me a chance to put a bid in. I don't know if I'm going to be able to hold my tongue when I see him tonight."

"Don't even give him the satisfaction of knowing he's got to you," Vera said. "If you think family loyalty or even common courtesy ever plays a part in Tom Rogers's business dealings, you are dead wrong. A tiger won't change its stripes, and Tom Rogers will always be a money-grubbing, selfish, inconsiderate bastard as far as I'm concerned."

"He'll get his comeuppance one day," Gladys said.

"Will he, though?" Jud said. "All the rest of us have been hit hard during these war years, but not him. He nickels and dimes everyone and keeps building his empire as if he were a Rockefeller. Wouldn't even give me a decent price for Dolly's foal last week. I might as well have given it to him. If I had no more to do with him it would suit me just fine, but it makes me so mad he wouldn't even offer me a chance to cut on his place. I wish we'd never bought land next to him. If we didn't live this close, I could pretend he didn't even exist."

"It's easy enough for me to pretend Helen doesn't exist," Vera said. "If she's darkened my door a dozen times since we moved into this house seven years ago I'd be surprised. She expects me to go there and help her every time you turn around, though. I go for the children, not for her. Those children are turning out real well, and it's no credit to their parents as far as I'm concerned. Sometimes I wonder if I had kept them when Elizabeth was born if Helen would have even noticed. She'd notice now for sure, since she barely lifts a finger to do a thing. She even has Dorothy Ferris in six days a week. Now you tell me why Helen would need a full-time housekeeper."

"What good is it getting all riled up over things right now?" Gladys interjected. "Let's just get going to the Pearl Hall and enjoy this lovely June evening. Best way to spite those two is just to show up there and dance up a storm. Nothing they have can hold a candle to what you two have worked so hard to build on this farm. And unless Lauren Bacall and Humphrey Bogart show up, you two are going to be the most stunning couple there."

As the three of them settled into an easy pace walking out the Neck Road and enjoying the beautiful evening, the rustling leaves swaying in the warm breeze filling the silence, Vera thought about what Gladys had said about her and Jud having more than Helen and Tom. She knew what Gladys was referring to and did feel a pride in what they had built together since the first summer in the tent. With hard work and thriftiness, they had managed to build a fine home, a substantial barn, and several outbuildings, and over time built up a good-sized herd. Jud was well respected when it came to the business of lumbering and could turn his hand to just about anything anyone needed done, which made him the first one called for odd jobs during the spring and summer months. She herself kept a lovely home, was active in the Women's Institute, was reputed to be the finest quilter around, and held a job she was proud of.

The aspiration she'd allowed herself to have so briefly was now so long ago that she rarely thought about it. The grief she'd felt when Austin drowned seldom entered her mind. She had been so young and naive. Becoming a nurse and living a life so different than the one she had now was not meant to be, probably even if Austin had lived. The life she had and the love between her and Jud was the life she was meant to have.

But Gladys had said *nothing* Helen and Tom had could hold a candle to what they had worked so hard for. That of course was not true. Henry, Margaret, and Elizabeth were more precious and valuable than any possessions, riches, or accomplishments. A family was the jewel in the crown, something they had not been blessed with. So much time had gone by and there had been so many disappointments and Vera seemed quite certain a family was the one thing she and Jud would never have.

1949

The sun beamed off the roof of Cecil Reid's long black car. The sunny, bright spring day did not seem fitting for what they had gathered at the Grey's Mills church to do. It had happened so suddenly. Joe Cronk had not shown any signs of poor health besides the deafness his family had gotten used to. He was still milking seven cows morning and night and it was the morning's bucket Marjorie had been waiting for that caused her to head to the barn to see what was taking him so long.

It was as if he had just fallen off the milking stool and instead of getting back up had decided to take a nap. He looked asleep when Marjorie first saw him. As she came closer and could see the somewhat distorted expression on his face she knew right away her husband was dead. Heart failure, Dr. Leatherbarrow said when he arrived from Hampton. Cecil Reid arrived minutes later.

Now the community was gathering to bury Joseph Henry Cronk. Neighbours remarked how strong Marjorie was, a rock they said. She had exhibited a stoic demeanour from the moment she'd found him until just minutes ago. But the act of getting out of her son-in-law's car and walking toward the crowd milling outside the small church seemed to have broken down whatever fortification had contained her emotions, and Marjorie Cronk was now sobbing uncontrollably. Vera Williams held one of her arms and Helen Rogers held the other as family members filed in behind them.

It was in this church fifty-two years ago to the very day Marjorie Bissett had married Joe Cronk. On this April day she would now have to say her final goodbyes. His body had been laid out in the parlour for the last two days, but it took walking into this church without him for the reality of Joe's death to hit her. Her husband was gone and the life they had together was over.

1953

Vera went to the veranda railing and hollered across the yard to Jud, "Can you come in and help me roll?" She walked back into the parlour and looked across at the Double Wedding Ring quilt on the wooden frames. The small pieces creating the intertwining circles were a kaleidoscope of colour. She was pleased with her choice for the quilting in the white kite-shaped and melon-shaped sections. A lot of quilting, but she was very happy with the overall effect. She had hoped to be finished by now, but going back and forth caring for Mother had given her little time for quilting. Perhaps with a full day at home she could at least get another roll or two and get closer to getting it off the frames. She might have to call some ladies in get some help if she was to get it finished in time for Margaret's wedding in December.

"That quilt's a piece of art, Vera. Margaret will be thrilled with it," Jud said.

"I don't have time to stand around looking at it. Get the clamps off on your end and pull that board tight as we roll. I'm going to quilt until around four and then go make supper for Mother. Maybe I'll be able to get a bite or two into her. I think she should be coming around better than she is. I'm going to get Dr. King to come back over if she hasn't rallied by tomorrow. You may as well get some lunch while you're in. There's still some roast chicken in the fridge."

"I'll grab a bite to eat when I get home. Len Woodbridge wants me to come have a look at the logs he has out to see if I think he has a load ready. It's a good thing I've got some guys loyal to their trucker. Tom's had trucks running steady over there, but of course he wouldn't think to offer a load or two to his brother-in-law. It's a wonder he has a tree left standing. I heard them talking about Tom's crew when I was at the store yesterday. Walter Whelpley quit on him, you know. Tom's got kids in there cutting and Walter says someone's going to get killed. He's cutting everything in sight."

"Yeah, I hear the saws running over there. He's started on the hill behind us. I thought for sure he'd stay off it where it's so steep. Never should have sold him Dolly's foal. He wouldn't get a tractor on a hill so steep, but he's got that young horse hauling wood off it like there's no tomorrow."

"Tom Rogers has no common sense if it interferes with making money, and for sure he isn't going to listen to anyone."

"I don't expect he will, but I'm stopping there on my way back from Len's. I'm going to tell him what I think of him getting truckers from town and I'm going to ask him not to cut so close to our line. It'll be an awful eyesore if he keeps going at the hill."

"Good luck. You may as well ask the sun not to set. That's more likely to happen than Tom Rogers giving up a dollar if there's one to be made. While you're at it, maybe you can mention to Helen her mother isn't well and might appreciate a visit from her. God forbid she actually help out."

Vera sat down and picked up her needle. She could get herself in an awful state when she thought about her sister. Marjorie Cronk had been sick all fall and not once had Helen offered to stay with her or help with her care. Three days ago, Helen had called Vera, inquiring about their mother's health.

"Is Mother feeling any better? I certainly hope she will be able to make Elizabeth's dress for Margaret's wedding. I don't want to have to pay a seamstress and I can't find anything in stores to suit her. I wish she was built like Margaret. Where she gets her girth is beyond me."

Vera had to bite her tongue whenever Helen started criticizing her youngest daughter's size. Helen herself had been a heavy child and should know firsthand just how hurtful people can be. In response to her sister's lament, Vera had offered to make Elizabeth's dress.

"Send Elizabeth over with the pattern and fabric this afternoon. I'll make her dress. She wanted to borrow some story books from me anyway. Jud and I love having her visit. She may as well stay for supper with us."

"Put another potato or two in the pot. I swear she eats more than a grown man. I tell her she should be losing her baby fat soon. She's already sixteen."

"I've got a pot boiling over," Vera said, cutting the conversation off to attend to the imaginary crisis.

Vera swiped at a tear to keep it from falling on the quilt.

She guided her needle, viewing her stitches through blurry eyes. She loved her sister's three children as if they were her own. She and Jud had stood in the auditorium for Henry's graduation two years ago and watched him receive his scholarship for the University of New Brunswick. What a fine young man he was.

Margaret was such a loving and kind girl. Over the years she had brought such joy to their home, always being so thoughtful and loving to her Auntie V and Uncle Jug, the names a two-year-old Margaret had given them. Vera wondered if this wedding, which was all Helen talked about, was more a result of Margaret being her accommodating, pleasant self than her finding the love of her life when her mother set her up with the Teed boy whose family summered in Clifton. Helen was thrilled with the union, hoping the social step up for her daughter would carry her upward as well. Vera was sure the big church wedding and fancy reception in Rothesay on Christmas Eve was all Helen's idea.

And then there was dear, sweet Elizabeth. She had spent most of her early years with Vera and Jud or her grandparents. Elizabeth had been an angel of a baby, hardly even crying and content to lie or sit for hours. Then once the darling little girl started walking, Helen got the notion her nerves were bad and having three children was more than her delicate state could cope with.

Three days ago, Elizabeth had burst into tears when Vera measured her for the dress.

"I am going to look hideous in this dress," cried Elizabeth. "I told Mom I wanted a style less poufy and frilly. I am going to look like a big pink marshmallow."

"Let's change the pattern a bit. We'll make it a more flattering dress and you'll look wonderful. We won't even show your mother until you put it on for the wedding."

"She won't notice anyway. She won't give me a look except to tell me how fat I am. Not a day goes by she doesn't make a comment about my size. It's what I put in my mouth, you know. That's the wisdom she offers me at every meal. I'm sure her own appearance and how beautiful Margaret looks will be her focus on the wedding day. Unless I come dressed in a burlap sack, she won't even notice me."

"You are a beautiful girl, Elizabeth. Don't let your mother's insensitivity bother you. She doesn't think before she speaks. Have you heard her go on about the grey in my hair lately? For some reason your mother feels the need to be the mirror she thinks we don't have."

Vera thought back to how hurtful Helen's first comments about her greying hair had been.

"There's some grey hair coming there, Vera. It sticks out in the dark head of hair you've always crowed about. You're not the young Vera Cronk who turned all the boys' heads anymore now, are you? And what a shame it seems that your childbearing years are coming to an end as well. What a sin God didn't see fit to give you and Jud a family."

Helen had said those words in a room full of ladies gathered in the Francis Smith Hall for the monthly W. I. meeting. Vera had gotten up quickly to attend to the tea and only Gladys saw the tears she was forcing back as she filled the cups in the kitchen.

"I think there's some rat poison under the sink if you'd like me to shake a little into your sister's tea," Gladys said as she stood next to Vera, her hand resting on her shoulder while Vera struggled to contain her emotions. "What makes her such a beast?"

Vera had done her best to comfort her niece. "Don't let her get to you, Elizabeth. Let her words fall off you like water off a duck's back."

"That's what Margaret says, Auntie V. But it's easy for her to say, she doesn't get the brunt of mother's meanness. 'Margaret's beautiful inside and out.' Another line I've heard all my life."

"You think Margaret doesn't get any of your mother's negative words, but she does. Margaret has worked like a little slave all her life trying to please your mother and nothing she does has ever been good enough. Each meal she makes lacks flavour or is over- or undercooked. There is always dust left behind or streaks on the kitchen floor. I've heard her go up one side of Margaret and down the other because the dishcloth wasn't soaked in Javex or the laundry wasn't hung on the clothesline correctly.

"But it's not my place to criticize your mother. Let's get this dress cut out and then we'll make supper. Maybe you could make those cheese biscuits your Uncle Jug loves so much. He'll be so happy to see you're joining us for supper."

Now Vera picked up the spool of quilting thread, snipped a new piece, then put it through the eye of her needle. Before sticking the needle into the fabric, she reached up and touched her hair. She was noticing more grey hair each time she looked in the mirror. She was showing her age. Her sister's words, though cruel and insensitive, were true. The reality of her childbearing years coming to an end was impossible to deny. The last three menstruation-free months were surely the beginning signs of her change of life and the final death knell to her dreams of welcoming a baby of her own into this house.

*

Vera stood beside Gladys as they dished up vegetables onto the plates. The supper was an annual event commemorating Armistice Day, and the Legion was a bustle of noise and activity, but a baby's cry could be heard above the clamour.

"My grandson is kicking up quite a fuss," Gladys said. "He wants to eat all the time. I hope his mother has enough milk for him. She may have to give in and put him on the Carnation. I don't go along with the new way of thinking. They're all saying the thing to do is to put babies onto the bottle. Breastfeeding is passé, they're telling mothers. Carnation milk and fancy glass bottles are the way to go. I just maintain the old way is the best way. Just feed him more often, I tell Barbara."

"Can you even believe you are a grandmother, Gladys?"

Vera said, lifting the lid off the roaster, the aroma of beef hitting her with a wave of nausea.

"You're not looking too good today, Vera. Are you feeling okay?"

"I've been a little squeamish lately. I think I'm feeling better when it hits me again. Certain smells seem to upset my stomach something terrible. I'm not losing any weight, though. I could barely fasten the waistband of this skirt this morning."

"Dorothy, can you take over for a few minutes? Vera's not feeling too well and I'm going to take her outside for some fresh air," Gladys said as she took Vera's arm and led her from the kitchen.

"I'm fine, Gladys," Vera protested.

When they got to the vestibule, Gladys sat Vera down and leaned in toward her. "I think you're pregnant, Vera. Have you missed your monthlies?"

"Don't be ridiculous, Gladys. I'm forty years old. I haven't menstruated for four months, but I just figured it was the change. Why would I get pregnant now after all these years?"

"I don't know the whys or wherefores, but I do know a pregnant woman when I see one. I believe you are at least four months along, further than you've ever gone before. You're going to feel this baby very soon if you haven't already felt something and just chalked it up to an upset stomach. You are going to be a mother, Vera Williams. I'd bet my life on it."

Vera covered her face with her hands, trying to take in the

truth of what her friend was saying. She'd had that thought briefly when she was getting dressed earlier but pushed the possibility right out of her mind. She was not going to allow herself to have such a foolish hope just to have it dashed. Gladys should know what she was talking about though after five pregnancies. Could she be right?

"We best get back in there and cut the pies," Vera said. "If Helen does it, the pieces will hardly be big enough to see. You'd think she was paying for the food, stingy as she is with her helpings. I'll call Dr. King in the morning and get over to see what this is. I am not going to get my hopes up until he tells me it's true. An old woman like me. Really, I'm not a character in a Bible story. John the Baptist's mother was really old, wasn't she?"

Gladys hugged her friend. "Yes, Elizabeth was old, and no, you're not a Bible story, Vera. But I believe you and Jud have been given a miracle."

"Keep your voice down, Gladys. I don't need anyone getting wind of this, especially before I know it's true. Too good to be true, I'm afraid."

*

Vera and Elizabeth sat in the waiting room of Dr. King's office. The room was crowded and noisy. A toddler right beside Vera was screeching and rubbing at her ear.

"I've tried everything," the mother said. "I even gave her a dose of paregoric and she's still fussing."

"I am so glad you let me come with you, Auntie V," Elizabeth said. "I am so excited to be in the room with you when you hear the news. It feels more like I'm going to be a sister than a cousin, but regardless I am going to love this baby to death."

"I am so nervous, Elizabeth. I just wish Dr. King could have told me the lab results over the phone. This is torture. I don't know what I'll do if I get in there and he tells me I'm not pregnant but just a foolish old woman believing the flutter of indigestion is a baby moving. I'll be embarrassed and heartbroken. I haven't even told your uncle. All the times we have been disappointed have been as hard on him as they have on me. He has long given up the idea there would be children. I wasn't putting him through it again."

"Mrs. Williams, the doctor will see you now."

*

"Let's go right to Waddell's and tell Uncle Jug," Elizabeth said as they drove off the ferry.

"I'm not going in and announcing my condition in front of a crowd of men. I will wait until he gets home."

"I don't know how you can wait. You didn't even tell Mrs. Carvell when you met her in the parking lot. She would have known something was up if she had been in the waiting room though. I am sure everyone heard you holler when Dr. King told you the good news. April. A baby in April. I've got to get knitting and you've got some sewing to do. Do you want a boy or a girl?"

"It makes no difference to me. I will be grateful and over-joyed if I carry this baby full term and God sees fit to bless us with a healthy baby."

*

"It almost looks comical, a woman your age in maternity clothes," Helen said.

"Oh, thanks so much for your support, Helen. But nothing you can say will take away my joy. Dr. King says I'm carrying a big, healthy baby, and I don't care if I have to wear a bedsheet by the end of it. I'll wear something respectable to Margaret's wedding if that's what you're concerned about. Don't you suppose those rich Rothesay ladies wear maternity clothes too, and perhaps even some are as old as I am?"

"Change-of-life babies are common, but it's your first."

"Is that a fact you think I'm not aware of? Do you have any idea how much I've longed for a baby all these years, Helen? I would think my own sister would be happy for me, not worried I was an embarrassment."

"I didn't say any such thing, Vera."

"Gladys and I are on our way to the quilting bee at the hall. I brought Henry those molasses cookies he's so fond of and I brought you a casserole. I expect you still have some last-minute things to do for the wedding."

"Oh, I do. Henry's going to drive Elizabeth and me across the river to meet Margaret. We need to finish decorating the hall. Gladys, you know all about weddings. All yours are married, aren't they? Imagine, Vera just starting a family. She's always got to be so different.

"I think Henry's in the shed with his father. On your way by, would you stop and tell Henry I'm waiting for him? I wanted Tom to take us over earlier, but God forbid he tear himself away from the place. He thinks if he leaves, the crew will slack off. I told him he should give the men the whole week off, but he thinks letting them knock off early Christmas Eve and having Christmas Day and Boxing Day off is more than generous of him."

"She is quite the piece of work, isn't she?" Gladys said as she and Vera walked across the yard.

"Oh, she's something, all right," Vera replied.

Vera and Gladys stopped a few steps away, hearing loud yelling coming from the tractor shed. The voices of Henry and Tom Rogers were clear, and even without opening the door they could make out the angry words the father and son were firing at each other.

"It's just greed, Father. I know you think I'm an idiot and I don't know what I'm talking about. You're going to get into trouble if you keep cutting on that hill. The whole base will be compromised."

"What the hell are you talking about? Is that some fancy book-learning term? I've been lumbering all my life. I think I know better than some wet-behind-the-ears, fancy college student."

"Dad, it's what I'm studying. I know you think being a

geologist is some pie-in-the-sky foolishness. 'All rocks and dirt,' you've said over and over again. But what the hell do you think is under your feet? Rocks and dirt. And the hill you are stripping bare has rocks and dirt and it will shift if you cut every tree down. The roots prevent erosion."

"Well, that shows how stupid you are. I'm not pulling the roots out. Those lame-brained cutters I've got in there don't even get right down to the base of the stump. I've got four-foot stumps in some spots."

"You don't get it, Dad. Living roots prevent erosion. The whole hill is clay on top of shale."

"How the hell would you know?"

"It's what I'm studying, Dad. Did you forget I got a scholarship? I'm not the dummy you've always thought I was."

"If you think you can come traipsing in here and tell me how to run my affairs, you've got another think coming. Go drive your mother and sister to Rothesay. I didn't hear you offer to do any work since you got here last night. I could have used your help loading this morning. Probably wouldn't want to get those lily-white hands of yours dirty."

"I'm not going to be a part of destroying that hill. Even if you don't believe what I'm saying, you could at least care enough about Aunt Vera and Uncle Jud not to create such a mess right beside their house."

"Oh, that's what this is about. Jud Williams put you up to this. He's been over here bellyaching ever since I started cutting that hill. It belongs to me and I'll damn well cut it if

I want to. You can tell them I said so, and after your sister's wedding you can stay the hell away from here. You'd think my own son would show me some loyalty."

Vera had no intention of stepping into the middle of this argument. She took Gladys by the arm and turned away. The two women slipped around the corner just as Henry bolted through the shed door, slamming it behind him.

1954

"If it's a boy I'm going to call him Keefe, Keefe Judson Williams. Don't bother telling me you don't like it, Gladys. Jud has given all his reasons against it, but I've made my mind up. I think honestly, though, he'd let me call this baby Fried Egg if I wanted to."

"Was Fried Egg a consideration?" Gladys asked.

"Very funny. I know Keefe is not a common name, but I stumbled on it in the baby name book Audrey lent me. As soon as I saw it I knew it was the name I would use. Keefe means cherished, and you tell me what little boy will be more cherished than this baby. I have waited a long time to hold a baby, and if it is a boy his name will be Keefe. To be honest with you, I haven't even come up with a girl's name. Somehow I just know it's a boy."

"Well, I'm not going to try to change your mind, Vera. It is my opinion children grow into whatever name they are given. I often wish my mother had thought better before using Gladys. And don't you think the name Gladys Titus hasn't been the brunt of many a joke. Keefe is no worse than lots of others. Would you want a baby named Horace or Percival? What about Maynard? The Donaldsons have named three generations of men Maynard. But when all is said and done, a name is just a name and you can name your baby anything you want to."

"Well, let's get to work and get this quilt off the frames this afternoon. Dr. King says it's a possibility I could go early, and I want everything ready before I go to the hospital. Elizabeth is upstairs helping Jud paint the small front bedroom. I've decided to put the baby in there. It's the warmest room because the chimney runs up through it. I know spring is nearly upon us but I want him in a nice cozy room next winter. I may as well put him in his own room right away. I don't go in with the notion of having the baby sleep in the room with us. I hope I hear him in the night from our room, though."

"Oh, you'll hear him all right. It's my experience a mother can hear her newborn almost before they make their first peep. You'll be right in synch, especially if you breastfeed. You are going to nurse this baby, aren't you?"

"I'm certainly going to try. It won't be from lack of breast size, I tell you. I'm surprised I can see the top of this quilt with these things in the way."

"It's so sad your mother died before getting to see her grandson," Gladys said.

"I know. At least she knew I was finally having a child and she got to go to Margaret's wedding. And it's good she only suffered in the hospital a short time. She would not have wanted to linger."

"It's a shame Henry didn't get home for the funeral," Gladys said.

"To hear Helen talk he was being self-centred and just stayed away to break his mother's heart. It wasn't the poor boy's doing. We heard his own father tell him to go and not come back. Pretty sure Tom isn't telling Helen that, though, when she goes on and on about her ungrateful, insensitive son. And did you happen to notice how Helen kept telling everyone at the funeral Margaret was so big because the doctor is sure she's carrying twins? Like it is the most shameful thing on earth she was pregnant when she got married. No chance of anyone thinking that about me. Even an elephant doesn't have a twenty-one-year pregnancy."

"Oh I know, to hear Helen go on you would think she has had the hardest life possible. I don't know how you stand her, Vera."

"I'm so happy these days I can stand just about anything. I barely give my sister a thought though. I've tried over the years and I can honestly say I haven't a thing to feel guilty about when it comes to her and Tom."

"You're right. Elizabeth is some excited about this baby and I would imagine she would rather stay right here with you and Jud if she had her druthers."

"Elizabeth is a darling girl. Don't know how I would have gotten through these years without Helen's kids. I love them as if they were my own."

"I know you do, Vera, but you just wait until the baby

comes. You won't have felt anything like what you'll feel when you hold a baby of your own."

"I believe love is love, Gladys, and we open our hearts for the children we're privileged enough to have in our lives. They bring the love with them, each and every one, and we get the blessing of it."

*

Jud took the sleeping infant from his wife's arms and passed him to Elizabeth. "I'm carrying you over the threshold again, Vera, and don't bother to fight me on it. This is a new home as far as I can see. It is a home for our son and for our family. We have waited a long time for this wonderful day and it is here. You, my love, have given me a strong, handsome son. Vera Williams, welcome home. Elizabeth, bring Keefe Judson Williams into his home and may he be blessed with a long and happy life."

"Aren't you the romantic fool? You'll put your back out carrying me," Vera laughed as Jud hoisted her into his arms. "Hurry up and get me through the door, then, and set me down. This handsome boy of yours will be hungry after you wake him with your foolishness. It's a wonder we're not soaked to the skin getting from the car, the way rain is coming down."

"April showers, all right, even if they started in mid-March," Jud said. "Surely this weather's going to change. The almanac never predicted this much rain."

"All right, set me down, Jud, and get out to the animals.

We'll get the fire going and start supper. You're a dear to come stay with me, Elizabeth. It means the world to have you share this time with me. It breaks my heart your grandparents passed before they got to see this boy. How was your mother when you told her you were coming to stay?"

"She wasn't thrilled with her maid coming next door. Dorothy Ferris quit a week ago, you know. How she has put up with Mother all these years is beyond me. You know how difficult Mother can be, and believe me she's been even worse since Grannie died and then with Margaret moving away. I think she thought Margaret and Gerald would live in Rothesay and she would have long stays with them. Gerald getting a job in Ottawa has not sat well with Mother. She would have gotten over the humiliation of Margaret being pregnant when they got married if she could have hobnobbed with Rothesay folk.

"And Father has been so cranky lately because this weather has stopped production, even with so few trees left to cut, especially on the hill behind your house. Anyway, I told them I was staying with you for a month. I can afford to stay home from school for a few weeks. My marks are good and missing a bit of time won't keep me from graduating. I did remind Mother about how much help you gave her when we were young. She of course did not offer to help out, so she really couldn't forbid me from coming."

"Well, I'm thrilled to have you here either way. I don't expect you to wait on me, but I love the company. We can enjoy this little treasure together. Isn't he just the most precious baby you've ever seen? I know I'm biased, but he is a perfect little boy, don't you think?"

"I think he is perfect, all right, but I'm probably a bit biased myself. Now you go lie down and I'll get the fire going and supper started. You should rest while he is sleeping. Don't even bother arguing with me. I am here to help you."

"How did I get so blessed with such a wonderful niece?"

"It is me who has been blessed. You have been the best aunt anyone could ask for. More like a mother to me, really. Anything I do for you is nothing compared to all you have done for me for as long as I can remember. If Keefe grows up loving me half as much as I love you, I will be thrilled."

"Oh, stop your flattery. I will go lie down, but I'm not an invalid. I just had a baby, for goodness' sake; I have not been stricken with a disease."

*

The loud rapping on the door woke Elizabeth. She hurried out of the downstairs bedroom to the front vestibule to keep the racket from waking Keefe and Vera. It was likely Uncle Jud was already in the barn, but it was still as black as night. She could not imagine who would be knocking at the front door at this early hour.

"Elizabeth, your mother has taken a bad spell and I need you to come home to care for her. She's been poorly for several days but she's not even making sense this morning. I can't care for everything. Surely Vera can spare you. The boy was born three weeks ago, was he not? She should be on her feet by now. Your mother needs you, and I'm not leaving without you. You can come for your things later. This rain has not let up. I could hardly get down the driveway for the gullies. Things are washing out something fierce."

"I can come over later once I get the fire going and breakfast underway. I don't want Vera to wake up to find me gone."

"Leave her a note, for God's sake. I don't have time to come back for you later. You can't walk in this. It's raining cats and dogs and the wind is ferocious. It's a gale. The power is likely to go out. I need you now and I don't expect I'll be able to get down this driveway much longer, if I can even get back up through the mud. Couldn't even get around to the back door. It's just a river of mud back there. Your mother is real poor and I might have to go for the doctor. I need you to come with me now. Surely you would help your own parents out. Vera and Jud will be just fine without you."

Elizabeth grabbed an envelope off the front hall table and jotted down a note for Vera. She would go tend to mother and be back as soon as possible. She grabbed her sweater and raincoat and slipped on her shoes. "Fine, I'll come with you now and see what Mother needs."

Tom Rogers watched as his daughter ran to the back door though the pouring rain. He had parked the truck as close to the house as possible. He had never seen such a wet spring. The culvert at the end of his driveway was overflowing and the water was across the road. The weather was probably the reason Helen was in such a state. It wasn't like she went outside much anymore, but these dark, rainy days were hard on everyone. He had no choice but to go get Elizabeth. Helen had been so agitated, especially at night, and he hadn't gotten much sleep in the last week.

How had his life come to this? It seemed nothing he did could calm Helen's aggression lately. Even with his height and weight advantage it was all he could do to fend off her physical attacks when she became agitated. He would ask Dr. King to increase her dosage. As difficult as it was to see her doped up, it was getting impossible to deal with her. He did not want to have to resort to sending her to the hospital. It was his job to care for her. His job, but if she continued this way he would have to consider committing her. For now, he would rely on Elizabeth's help. Henry and Margaret had abandoned them. And Vera, who had always helped out, was now busy with her newborn. Surely things would settle down and surely this damn rain would stop soon.

*

Driving conditions were terrible, but Dr. King arrived in the afternoon and stated Helen Rogers had had a psychotic break-down and shouldn't be left alone. The telephone lines were down as well, so Elizabeth could not even call Aunt Vera to tell her she wouldn't be returning for a few days.

"Oh, for goodness' sake stop your fretting, Elizabeth," Tom Rogers barked. "Vera is perfectly capable of managing without you. You would think you would be feeling guilty for having left your mother and her ending up in this state. If she'd had your help these last few weeks she might not have gotten in such a frenzy. I don't want to hear another thing about Vera or that cursed baby. Once this storm is over you can run over and see them, but for now you are where you are most needed."

Elizabeth had taken to her own bed after settling Mother down for the night. The howling wind and driving rain filled her with a foreboding she could not shake. Finally, after a lot of tossing and turning she fell into a deep sleep.

*

Vera hadn't noticed the note at first. She was surprised Elizabeth wasn't in the kitchen when she came downstairs and that it had been Keefe's cry that woke her up. Usually at the first sound he made Elizabeth was right in the room to get him up, change his diaper, and then bring him to Vera's bed for his morning feeding. He was a dream of a baby. Not one bit fussy or colicky. If his first three weeks were any indication, he was going to be an easy baby.

When Elizabeth hadn't been in the kitchen and the fire was just coals from when Jud had started it hours before, Vera had gone into Elizabeth's room. Her bed was unmade. She walked into the vestibule. The umbrella was missing from the hall tree. She saw the note on the front hall table.

Aunt V, Father came to get me. He says Mother is not
well and needs me to attend to some things. I will try to
get back as soon as possible. Give Keefe a big kiss for me.

Love Elizabeth

*

Vera hoped Jud would have no trouble on the bus run this
nasty day. A couple of the back roads were already closed due
to washouts. She had never seen such a wet spring. These last
three weeks would have been so much drearier if Elizabeth
had not been here to keep her company. She shouldn't mind
her leaving for a few hours and she was perfectly capable of
getting on without her. Vera wondered what Elizabeth meant
by her mother not being well. There was a lot of cold and flu
going around. Gladys's whole family had come down with it
and Jud said he had heard of several other folks being ill as
well. Perhaps that is why Tom came to get Elizabeth.

Vera had been concerned about Helen lately. Maybe she
should never have let Elizabeth leave her mother to come stay
with them. God knows Helen could be a handful and Tom
Rogers seemed quite capable of handling her moods. His
handling was the problem as far as Vera could see. Tom gave
in to her, let her have her outbursts, catered to her strange
moods.

Her parents had catered to Helen for years too. If they had
stood up to Helen's foolishness, perhaps she would have made

more of an effort. Her first really bad stretch was a full year after the drowning. Helen became obsessed with the church, spending the entire summer going back and forth to Beulah. She was almost hysterical most of the time. She kept saying her soul was headed for the fires of Hell. She barely ate, hardly slept, and ended up by the end of August taking to her bed for weeks. And then as quickly as her bad spell had started, she was out of bed and giving all her attention to Tom Rogers and the planning of her June wedding.

Helen had treated her own children terribly. Not much wonder Henry had left after Margaret's wedding and Margaret had been happy to move away. Mother's own health after Father died had deteriorated mainly from worry over Helen. Maybe it was time to step in and convince Tom he should demand more than just pills from the doctor. Helen's problems needed looking into.

Vera set her bread dough and decided if the rain stopped she would bundle up the baby and head over to check on things next door. Perhaps she and Elizabeth could talk some sense into Tom. Maybe Helen needed to go to the hospital on the west side of Saint John. It wasn't such a shameful thing these days to seek help for such things. In the long run, it would be better for everyone if Helen were to get some treatment for her problems.

The rain did not let up all morning. By midafternoon the power had gone out. Luckily there was enough dry wood in the porch to keep a hot fire going and Vera had cooked her two loaves of bread and a pan of rolls. The afternoon was dark and dreary. When Keefe went down for his nap Vera lay down for a spell too. Surely the sun would come out one of these days. Things would look more hopeful when the sun came out.

Vera and Jud ate their supper by candlelight. Keefe seemed a bit fussier than usual.

"I think he misses Elizabeth," Jud said.

"Me too," Vera replied. "I found today the longest day ever. I didn't know just how much her sunny disposition lights this house up. Were you here when Tom came to get her?"

"I met him on the road. I left the truck up at the mailbox tonight. The driveway is washed out badly near the top."

"There's a lot of mud at the back door too. It's going to be quite the mess to clean up if it doesn't stop raining soon."

"I know. That hill is washing out something terrible. After this storm, I'm going over to have it out with Tom. There's not much he can do now, but I want him to come have a look at the mess the hill is in. If I have to get a backhoe in to fix things I'm sending him the bill. Ernie said it's supposed to clear tomorrow. Thank goodness. Hopefully this mess of weather will be behind us. It's going to put the planting back a bit, I can tell you. But on the upside, there will be some extra work to be had, fixing up the roads. Why don't you head to bed early? Go when you put the baby down. It's going to be a long, dark, and nasty night. Get a good night's sleep and maybe when you wake up tomorrow the sun will be shining."

"I think I will. I don't feel like having our evening domino game with Elizabeth not here to play with us. Keefe didn't sleep very long this afternoon so I think he'll settle quickly. I might just let him sleep in our room tonight, right in bed with me. It goes against my better judgement but I don't want to have to tramp through the dark to his room if he wakes in the night. I've been spoiled with Elizabeth at my beck and call. I'd feel better having him close by tonight with the way the wind's still howling."

"Sounds like a good idea, Vera. I'll sleep in the back bedroom and leave you two alone tonight. Must say I'm looking forward to the day when sleeping beside my wife returns to normal, but for now our precious son is what matters. What more could a man ask for than to see his beautiful wife sleeping peacefully beside his baby boy?"

"We are some blessed, Jud Williams. This little guy was well worth the wait. What more on earth could we ask for?"

*

Sunshine was streaming in the window when Elizabeth awoke late the next morning. She jumped up with a start. At first she thought she was in the small bedroom at Aunt Vera and Uncle Jud's but then remembered she was in her own room at home. Thank goodness the storm had passed, this sunshine the first there had been for weeks. She would attend to Mother quickly and then make her way over next door to see how they had weathered the storm. She could hardly wait to hold Keefe. Being separated from him for even this short time had been torturous.

Elizabeth walked into the kitchen to find Father and two of his lumbering crew sitting at the kitchen table. Gladys Titus was also there, which seemed very odd to Elizabeth, since Mother and Gladys were far from being friends.

"There's been a terrible thing happen, Elizabeth," Gladys said. "The baby survived. A miracle, really. They took him to Mrs. Whelpley's. We can go get him shortly, but I wanted to tell you what happened first before they brought him here. Vera and Jud are gone."

"What do you mean, gone?" Elizabeth stuttered, leaning against the sideboard. "What are you talking about?"

"It was an avalanche. An avalanche of mud and rocks," Percy Johnston said. "The hill came down and broke the house to pieces just as if it were made of toothpicks. I've never seen the like of it."

Tom Rogers sat in silence, his face set like stone, and made no move to comfort his daughter.

Percy kept talking. "It knocked Jud down on the back stairs, we think, and covered him like lava. They haven't found Vera yet but she must have made it to the front. She threw the infant out a window, we gather. It's a wonder we found the little one. It was the blue of his blanket I saw. He was just lying there on the veranda roof. The veranda came right off, broke right off in one piece. How that baby stayed on that roof is beyond me. A miracle, I'd say."

"And it's a miracle, Percy, you got there when you did, or the baby might have died too," Dave Evans added, turning to Elizabeth. "Percy was dropping feed off to Jud and wasn't even going to go in the driveway, it's washed out so bad, but something told him he should. I can't even imagine finding such a thing."

Gladys crossed the room and wrapped her arms around Elizabeth, who had not made a sound. She stared straight ahead with a look that chilled Gladys to the bone. *This poor, dear girl,* thought Gladys. How cruel to break such ghastly news in such a way, but what choice was there? The horror of what had happened could not be avoided.

"We'll go get Keefe. He will need you to be strong, Elizabeth. Sit a spell and get yourself together," Gladys said.

"To think a night brought such wreckage and the sun's shining this morning as if nothing happened," Dave Evans said. "It's a damn shame is what it is. Who would have thought such a thing could happen?"

Elizabeth got up from her chair and walked across the room. She stood inches away from her father, and with a tone as steady and cutting as a diamond, she spoke: "Henry thought such a thing could happen. Henry told you, Father, and you would not listen." She turned toward Gladys. "Take me to get Keefe."

*

Elizabeth walked up the road trying to manoeuvre the carriage along the uneven dirt shoulder. The small granite marker she had finally convinced Father to purchase to mark the graves had been put in place a week ago, and this morning was the first time she had could get away to come see it. The September day was warm, and Keefe was sound asleep, curled up comfortably in the carriage.

She could have put him down in his crib for his nap and walked to the Long Reach graveyard alone, but she wasn't sure Mother would go to the baby if he were to wake up while she was gone. Mother would hold Keefe now and again but never tended to his needs. Father didn't even acknowledge Keefe's existence other than making clear his resentment about the cost of caring for him.

"I suppose you think we're going to pay someone to look after this baby while you go gallivanting off to Modern Business College in the city. Bad enough I have to pay your tuition. I'm not dishing out any more money, so I guess you'll just have to stay put and earn your own and his keep. I expect someone would want him if we let it out he's up for adoption. There don't seem to be anything wrong with him, although it might take a while before they can tell if he's mental or anything from the fall he had."

"There isn't anything wrong with him, Father. He's growing just fine. I already called the college and told them I wasn't entering this fall. Keefe's not going anywhere as long as I am around. We're the only family he has, the poor little fellow. Maybe when he starts school I'll be able to go to college then."

"School? We're not keeping him until he starts school. This isn't the Protestant Orphanage Home. It's not up to us to keep him."

Elizabeth thought back to the comment she made on the way out the door. She wasn't sure if her father heard her accusation. Who else should it be up to, to keep the baby who lost his parents in such a tragic and preventable way? Over the last four months Elizabeth had made it perfectly clear she held her father responsible for what had happened to her aunt and uncle.

"Stop making your father so upset," Mother had said yesterday. "He won't take your disrespect much longer. He already sent Henry away and Margaret moved away from his hatefulness. Watch your mouth or he'll send you away, and then where will I be?"

"Always worried about number one, aren't you, Mother? What about this tiny boy who has no parents to care for him? What about your own flesh and blood? Your sister is dead, or have you even bothered to notice? This is the precious boy she waited so long to have, and three weeks later she dies. I would think anyone with any compassion at all would vow to do their very best to give this baby the life she would have made sure he had."

"I'm not well, you know. Dr. King has increased my pills and he says I should stay away from anything upsetting."

"You've stayed away from facing anything for as long as I can remember, including lifting a finger to run this house.

Maybe if you'd done your part, Henry would not have left and Margaret would have wanted to live in the same province."

"What a mean thing to say, Elizabeth. Vera filled your head with nasty ideas and disrespect for your own parents."

"She did no such thing. She always made me feel loved and special. Any confidence I have, Aunt Vera gave me. She gave me back what your judgement stripped from me. This baby is the only thing keeping me from succumbing to the terrible grief I feel. You and Father don't seem to have an ounce of feeling about anything but yourselves."

"I must lie down. Your words are cruel. How can you not see how weak I am?"

Elizabeth pushed the carriage up the steep path, parking it in the shade of the large oak tree in the graveyard. She walked over to the marker. Tears streamed down her cheeks as she read the names etched on the granite stone. She was in such misery. The people she loved most in this world had been taken so suddenly, in such a horrific way. Would anything have been different if she had been there? Would there be a marker here with her name on it as well if she hadn't left with Father that day? She needed to stay strong for this precious baby, but what hope did she have of escaping life under her parents' roof? What did the future hold for her and Keefe? The words she fired at her parents daily echoed a strength she did not truly feel. Was she more like her mother than she was willing to admit? What would happen to this small boy if she were to give in to the deep anguish she fought every waking hour and the terror her nightmares brought her when she finally slept?

*

Elizabeth's head jerked toward the sliver of light she could see through the small window near the ceiling. Terrified, she tried to lift herself off the mattress but met the resistance of straps securing her arms and legs to the narrow bed. Her eyes quickly adjusted to the dim light and she took in her surroundings. She struggled again but to no avail. She quieted her breathing to take in the noises she could hear. It sounded as if a heavy door was being shut. She could hear moaning and hollering and the sound of a floor waxer. Her dry mouth felt like wool socks. Where was she and how had she gotten here?

The door creaked open and a woman in a starched white uniform entered the small room, her presence looming above the bed.

"You are finally waking up, Miss Rogers. We thought you were hibernating for the winter. I'm your nurse, dear. You can call me Bea."

Elizabeth bobbed her head violently from side to side. "Where am I? Let me up. I need to look after Keefe."

"You calm right down, dear. You are in no state to look after anyone. If you calm down I can untie your arms and prop you up so you can have some broth. I need to get you on the bedpan too so I don't have to change your bedclothes again."

Elizabeth lay still, trying to gather her wits about her. She could not remember arriving at this place. She couldn't re-member anything. Who was looking after Keefe? She cried out his name, raising her head again.

"Just relax, dear. Your medication will be coming soon and I want to get some nourishment into you before they put you out again. Now, if I unbuckle these straps, are you going to cooperate? I will bring in an orderly to help me if you don't, and you won't get anywhere fighting Harold, I can tell you."

Elizabeth lay perfectly still as the nurse unfastened her constraints. Tears ran down her cheeks. Perhaps this was a bad dream and she would soon wake up in her own bedroom, Keefe asleep in his crib across the room. She squeezed her eyes shut, hoping for the familiar noises of a regular morning at home to greet her. The cold metal bedpan jolted her back to the reality of this nightmare and the knowledge she was wide awake.

*

A different nurse propped Elizabeth up and passed her a small cup of water. Sipping some, she swallowed the pill. Moments earlier her attempt to leave the room had been quashed by the large man. He had blocked her exit and led her back to the bed, not cruelly but certainly with the message she was not to try to leave this small room again. Bea had fastened her leg straps but kept her arms free.

"Let your medication work, dear. You must rest if you are going to get better. You are more lucid than when you arrived.

Just let the pill relax you. No one is going to hurt you, dear."

Elizabeth turned her head and settled into the scratchy pillow. She closed her eyes, drifting a bit while flashes of memory pushed into her foggy brain.

The cold November wind was blowing the skiff of snow that had fallen in the night. She had put Keefe down for his morning nap and had bundled up to go for a walk, hoping to clear her troubled thoughts, the nightmare still so vivid in her mind. In the months following that terrible night she had not even walked by the driveway. She had had no intention of walking in but had rushed down the driveway, pulled toward the sound as a second shot rang out.

Elizabeth opened her eyes, trying to resist the grogginess and the wave of helplessness she was feeling. Dolly. She could see her uncle's horse on the ground, red blood staining the white snow.

1955

Tom Rogers backed his half-ton as close to the corner as he could. This morning he would at least try to do what Helen had been harping at him to do for months. It was hard to believe a year had gone by already. He had only been here once since the day poor Elizabeth had happened upon him shooting that damn horse. What followed still haunted him. Some days he wished there had been another bullet in the shotgun.

Helen started on about the hall tree shortly after Elizabeth had gone into the hospital. She barely even said a word about her daughter's absence, but she could not seem to stop thinking about her mother's hall tree being in Vera's house. She still talked about Vera's house with anger and resentment.

"She got a brand-new house. I had to move into this old falling-down shack. Nothing but the best for Vera. Why Mother gave her the hall tree, I don't know. I always said how fond I was of it. She knew I wanted it. Vera knew too, which is why she dragged the old thing to her new house."

Again, this morning she had gone into a tangent about the hall tree. "Don't know why I can't have it now," she said over and over at breakfast. Helen had no idea what the house she had been so jealous of looked like now. The back wall had been completely knocked out, filling the back stairs with mud and debris. It was thought Jud had been caught on the back stairs during the full force of things. When the back wall fell in it caused the roof to shift violently and split the house in half as if an earthquake had demolished it. The middle beam was thought to have struck Vera as the top storey collapsed, causing the front veranda to hit the ground below.

Entering the ruined house after such destruction and with it being exposed to the elements of the last year was treacherous enough, and it somehow seemed intrusive and disrespectful. Nothing had been touched. All of Vera and Jud's possessions lay strewn about in the ruins. The hall tree was probably destroyed, but he would attempt to find it in the rubble. It would serve him right if the remaining structure fell in and suffocated him. Would Helen still grieve for the damn hall tree when she was told he had died retrieving it for her?

*

Weekly, Elizabeth would sit in the small office across from Dr. Gregory and listen to his long deliberation regarding her condition. He would begin by going over the behaviours of her past week, listing the changes she had to make if she wanted to eventually be released.

"Your parents are very concerned for your well-being and worry your violent behaviour might cause you to harm yourself or someone else. We will continue with the drug regime we have you on and your monthly shock treatments. You have got to quiet the demons in your head and accept your treatment if you are to get better. Your parents want what is best for you."

Elizabeth bit the inside of her cheek, forcing herself to contain the thoughts boiling in her head. It was torture to hear this man go on about her parents' concern for her well-being. They had put her in this place, separating her from the only thing she had to live for. In the last few months in this prison she had periods of severe agitation, her angry outbursts resulting in Harold and Bea strapping her to her bed for days at a time. She had also had long stretches of being nearly catatonic when she would lie in bed praying for any opportunity to end this misery. She had gotten to her current numb state, determined to cooperate and do everything she was told, on the day she realized it was Keefe's first birthday. She now recorded each day's date in her small notepad, consciously thinking of doing everything possible to convince the doctors she was better so she would be released to care for Keefe again.

"We think perhaps you are now well enough to start working a couple of days a week in the laundry. This would give you a purpose and something to fill your time. If you are going to be well enough to return home, you need to begin to show the ability to carry out simple tasks. We will start you out folding towels. Do you think you could do that, Elizabeth?"

Elizabeth nodded her head and produced a witless smile,

thinking that reaction to be the most beneficial. This man didn't care anything about her getting better or returning home. She would fold towels all day long, every day for as long as it took. She would do whatever she needed to do to get back to Keefe. But would he even remember her when she got out of this place?

1957

Elizabeth wrote the date in her notepad as she prepared for bed. January 19, 1957. The two years and two months she had spent here had dragged by, each day a carbon copy of the one before. She had not even been outside, feeling no fresh air, heat, sun, or the cold wind whipping up off the roiling water of the Reversing Falls. But she could see the falls churning below when she looked out the small barred windows. Bea had told her early on that she would be here indefinitely. Her committal had been court ordered. She had tried to kill her father.

He'd hit her with the gun butt after she had fallen to the ground. Was his daughter such a threat to him he had to render her unconscious to subdue her? He and two other men had loaded her into the back of Father's Sedan Delivery and brought her here. Delivered her to this prison without even letting her pack some things or say goodbye to Keefe.

It was torture wondering every day how Keefe was doing. Who was caring for him? The torture had almost caused her to completely give up before she found the determination to survive this hell so she could get back to him. She had done everything they asked of her. She accepted the treatment and offered no resistance. After months of managing menial tasks she had moved on to running the large ironer and had recently been given the responsibility of supervising all the laundering.

During the daytime amid the routine and familiar order in the laundry Elizabeth could keep her mind calm and focused. When she entered the facility, she could even imagine herself arriving at a regular workplace and found some satisfaction in that scenario. But during the long evenings followed by hours of sleeplessness, listening to the sounds of suffering and agony around her, she would struggle to keep from giving in to the feelings of desperation and hopelessness. How long would they keep her here? What more could she do than what she was already doing to convince them she should be released from this place?

*

The laundry was shut down for Christmas Day. The ward was decorated and the staff who had been required to work were attempting to appear festive. Bea was wearing a Santa hat when she entered the room and sat down beside Elizabeth's bed.

Over Elizabeth's time in Centracare, Bea Smith had become a friend, not just her nurse. Elizabeth knew how fortunate she was to have been placed in the ward where Bea worked. She'd had contact with many other nurses but none like the kind, warm-hearted Bea Smith. Some other nurses seemed to take pleasure in adding to the patient's misery, certainly doing nothing to alleviate it. But even when Bea had had to subdue or control Elizabeth's behaviour she had never done it in a mean or heartless manner.

"I think you can apply to the review board in the new year to have your committal rescinded," Bea said.

"What do you mean?" Elizabeth asked.

"Well, things are changing quite a bit around here. With the new administration and a new focus on patient care, the objective is toward outpatient care. The system used to be perfectly suited to keeping patients in the facility long term. Some patients have been here for most of their adult lives. Things are changing to give patients more rights and more control over their own futures."

"I can't imagine how anyone could keep going with no hope of getting out of this place. Seeing Keefe again is the only thing keeping me from giving up. Tell me more about how this application could help me get out of here."

"Well, you have reached the mandatory minimum requirement documented when you were admitted. You have a consistent and lengthy good behaviour record and have shown responsibility in your work placement. I could write a letter of recommendation to accompany your application. The review board would look at all these things and consider outpatient care either on a permanent or trial basis."

"Would my parents be consulted? Could they interfere with my release? They haven't even visited or bothered to write to me. I think they are perfectly happy to have me here. My sister has written a few times and a neighbour sent me the only photograph I have of Keefe. He will be a much bigger boy by the time I get to see him again. Margaret assures me he is being looked after, but how she knows for sure, I don't know. Mother and Father can tell her anything over the phone. Would I get a chance to talk to this review board and plead my case?"

"It is a lengthy process and won't happen overnight. They consider your overall well-being and the danger you present to yourself and others. With your good record and the amount of time you've been here, they're likely to at least give you a conditional discharge. Surely your parents would be supportive of your release?"

"One would think so, wouldn't one? But of course one would think most parents would want the best for their own flesh and blood. I'm afraid that's not the case with my parents. But I must put my worry aside and do everything I can to get out of here. Once I get out and get Keefe, then I'll find a way to get out of their grip."

"God love you, Elizabeth. I will certainly do all I can to help. You have suffered enough. I will speak to the head nurse and get the paperwork you need to get things started. Maybe by the time your little cousin has his fourth birthday you'll be back home to celebrate it with him. Now, try to perk up and enjoy the day. They have the dining room all decked out, and I believe they're even serving plum pudding with your Christmas dinner. Fresh turkeys from the peninsula, I hear, and all the fixings."

1958

The proceedings of Elizabeth Rogers's first release hearing were straightforward and the first three witnesses were positive and supportive. They spoke of the progress Elizabeth had made, and as she sat watching the reactions of the release board to what each witness presented, Elizabeth finally allowed herself to believe she would be home for Keefe's birthday.

Everything appeared to be going in Elizabeth's favour until the social worker read a letter from Helen Rogers explaining her reservations regarding her daughter returning home. She stated her daughter's condition put her and her husband's life in danger. She also wrote about her concern regarding the safety of her young nephew and the upset it would cause him to have an unstable person in the home. In the short discussion following the letter, the board ruled Elizabeth Rogers not fit for release at this time.

Upon hearing the ruling Elizabeth experienced shortness of breath and an anxiety attack so severe she was sure it was going to kill her. She was inconsolable. Bea and Harold as well as several other staff members watched her for twenty-four hours, comforting her as best they could. She had to be sedated, and it was five days before she was able to speak about the trauma of her mother's words and the hateful intent behind them.

The first hearing took place on April 1, and Elizabeth went into it hoping she would be released and back home in time for Keefe's fourth birthday. She saw the date as a good omen; it wasn't until two weeks later she considered the April Fool aspect.

"April Fool's Day. I was the fool to believe everything I worked so hard at to bring about my discharge could not be wiped out by my mother's hatred. I should have known she would find a way to keep me here. Perhaps she is right, Bea. The way I feel about her right now, I would be capable of killing her—and my father too, as he must have gone along with her. It is the cruel lie about Keefe's well-being I am most haunted by. To hear her voice such concern for a child she barely even acknowledged makes my blood boil. Unless she has changed completely, I am quite certain his well-being barely enters her mind. I can only hope Father has at least hired someone to look after him. Surely even they could not have a child suffer neglect under their roof."

The second hearing was scheduled for June 30. A psychiatrist, new to the hospital, had taken it upon herself to plead Elizabeth's case and presented her findings to the release board, stating Elizabeth Rogers presented no danger and was deemed competent and ready to return to society. With no letter from Helen Rogers or anyone else stating the contrary, the board ruled in favour of release. The doctor would continue treatment on an outpatient basis.

On July 1 Bea helped Elizabeth pack up her few belongings and walked her outside to where Tom Rogers was waiting to drive his daughter home.

"You will be just fine, Elizabeth," Bea said as she hugged Elizabeth goodbye. "I want you to call me whenever you need to. You are strong and you will manage. Once you see Keefe you will be able to get through whatever happens. You can do this."

Elizabeth looked over to see her father standing beside a vehicle she did not recognize. A new vehicle, from the look of the glistening black paint and shiny silver chrome. He looked older, his hair and beard grey, almost white. He looked thinner and more stooped than she remembered. She was sure he would find her appearance had changed drastically as well. Mother would not be able to criticize her weight, anyway. The dress she had been wearing when she arrived hung on her as if she were Aunt Vera's wire dress form, and the several hospital-issued shift dresses were in varying sizes. The wincey dress she wore today would certainly not have fit her three years ago.

Elizabeth stifled a laugh, thinking she could present her stay in Saint John's Centracare as a weight-loss vacation getaway. A spa retreat like she used to see advertised in her mother's *Woman's Day* magazines. Elizabeth also stifled her deep and seething anger as she approached her father. He had not so much as sent a birthday card, let alone stopped by on visitors' days. It wasn't as if she expected either one of her parents to make an effort to see her or keep in touch, but here he was, picking her up as if her time away had not been his fault. What could he possibly say to erase the misery of her years of confinement and imprisonment behind the locked doors of this place?

And what could she say? She knew if she pulled out the stop and released the anger boiling and churning below the surface of her calm and controlled demeanour, the orderlies who stood at the door watching her discharge would quickly escort her back into the hospital.

No, she would not succumb to the anger. She would quietly get in this fancy new car and silently resume her role as the dutiful daughter. She would suppress her true feelings so she could reunite with the most important treasure Aunt Vera and Uncle Jud had left behind. She would care for their beloved son and she would not allow her pain to jeopardize that again.

The drive home was overwhelming. It seemed so foreign to see the outside world as it rushed by through the car window. Her fear was almost choking her, but she kept focused on the destination, which would take her to Keefe. He would not be the baby she remembered, but she was determined to somehow pick up where their separation had left and put all her attention and energy into loving Aunt Vera's precious boy.

"Your mother is not good," Tom Rogers said as he pulled into the yard and turned the engine off. "She's been real bad the last month or so. She's looked after the boy as best she could but she can't have him underfoot. He's been looked after, though, so don't go accusing her of nothing. She'll end up in the place you just came from if you push her. She's delicate and I won't have you riling her up."

Elizabeth did not even respond. She only cared about Keefe and her desperation to see him increased exponentially with her father's warning, which seemed to be some explanation for what she might find inside the house.

Elizabeth noticed the quiet first. The kitchen looked the same as the day she had left except it was possibly starker, almost as if no one actually lived there. She walked into the hall and her father walked behind her.

"He's in there. Now don't you go getting mad. I just put him in there so I could go get you. I couldn't have him wandering around the house and your mother wasn't up to watching him."

Elizabeth opened the door to the small bedroom off the downstairs hall. The smell hit her first and then her eyes went to the corner where the boy sat, not even able to stand up in the contraption that had converted the old crib into a cage. A gasp escaped from her mouth, and when she turned around she saw her father had disappeared. She heard the kitchen door slam.

Elizabeth rushed toward the bed, pulling back the toggle and releasing the wire frame that sat atop the crib. She threw back the cover and reached in, pulling the boy up into her arms.

"Keefe, you precious boy. You darling, precious boy. I am so sorry. I am so sorry."

Elizabeth's suppressed emotions came flooding out as she slumped to the floor, cradling the boy. Her gasping sobs sounded foreign. She had so carefully contained even a tear in the last year, always mindful of appearing completely in control. This release was terrifying and as her sobs escaped, Elizabeth was overcome.

It was Keefe's small hand reaching up to touch her face that brought Elizabeth back from the precipice her pent-up pain had threatened to push her over. Elizabeth calmed her crying, released Keefe from her embrace, and set the boy down beside her, surveying his condition. His clothes were filthy and it appeared as if he had been soiled for quite some time. She looked around the room, stood, and walked over to a small dresser. She opened the top drawer, finding some diapers and a few items of clothing. She was not going to wrestle a cloth diaper onto this big boy. She would bathe him first and then set about to teach him to use the toilet. Whatever challenges toilet training might bring, it would be better than having him sit in his own waste.

Elizabeth sat back down beside the boy, scooping him up again into her arms. "You are a precious boy," Elizabeth kept reciting, trying to keep her voice quiet and soothing, not allowing the rage she felt distract her from the comfort she was determined to offer this poor, frightened child.

"I'm going to give you a bath, dolly boy. A nice warm bath, and then Elizabeth will put some clean clothes on you. Don't be scared. Elizabeth will take care of you."

Tears were streaming down her cheeks, and she kept wiping at them, trying to hold in her anguish. It would frighten the boy more if she were to lose her composure again.

She set him down and stood up again. There was much to be done. This child had to be loved and cared for. Her words and actions would rebuild the horrible damage neglect had done to this precious child.

"Are you hungry, dolly boy? After your bath Elizabeth, will make you something good for your lunch."

As she picked him up again, the expression on his face quickly turned to fear. He let out a panicked cry.

"Don't worry, dolly boy. I'm not putting you back in there. You never have to go back in there again. Elizabeth is here now. Elizabeth will look after you."

An hour later, after she had given Keefe a bath, dressed him, and gotten him something to eat, Elizabeth attempted to rip the wire frame from the crib. It had been securely nailed on and after only budging one corner she gave up. Keefe was squatting in the far corner of the room, not crying but emitting a low whimper. Elizabeth picked him up and he clung to her. With her free arm, she took hold of the crib and dragged it from the room. It barely fit through the hallway, but she managed to get it out the front door, where she pushed it out onto the veranda, and while still holding Keefe tightly she kicked it down the five front steps. The sides of the rickety old crib collapsed when it hit the ground.

1959

Elizabeth and Keefe walked into Union Station while Tom Rogers parked the car. Margaret's train was scheduled to arrive in fifteen minutes. The parked trains Keefe had seen outside on the tracks as they drove up filled him with excitement. Elizabeth picked him up and stood him on the wooden bench, giving him a clear view of the track and platform where Margaret and the children would be coming on a moving train very soon.

"For my birthday?" Keefe asked.

"Yes, Dolly boy, for your birthday."

Keefe's speech had grown in leaps and bounds from the guttural, unrecognizable sounds he was making when she returned home nine months ago. His simple sentences, usually consisting of only a few words, might to an observer seem far below what a five-year-old should be saying, but Elizabeth knew he was making excellent progress considering the circumstances of his first four years. She swelled with pride every time he opened his mouth to speak. Despite what the poor child had been through, he was a smart, attentive, and delightful child.

"The train, Lizbeth. The train coming!"

*

Helen Rogers was leaning against the unlit wood stove in the kitchen when Elizabeth, Margaret, and the children walked in. "Well, look what the cat drug in," she said. "I came down and not a coal in this damn stove. I hollered for your father but no one answered me. I thought the rapture had taken place. Left behind, I thought. This is hell and I'm left here to suffer."

"Dad and I both told you we were going into the city to pick Margaret and the children up at the train. I have been telling you for days they were coming. Look at the children, Mother. Haven't they changed a lot from the pictures Margaret sent last? They are growing so quickly. Look how tall Jason is, Mother."

"I'm not a fool, Elizabeth. I realize children grow. Please don't treat me like an imbecile. I am the *mother* in this house. Are you going to start this damn fire and get a meal prepared? It's a wonder I don't starve to death."

Margaret took her mother's arm and led her from the room. "I'll take you up to bed, Mother. The children are anxious to get out and see the animals. Maybe you will have more energy to visit with them after a rest and a good supper. Elizabeth got Father to stop at the City Market for pork chops. She'll have a delicious supper made in a jiffy. We're having birthday cake for Keefe. Can you believe he's turning five, Mother?"

"Don't you start criticizing me like your sister. I can't be expected to look after the boy. He's not ours. Why Vera had a baby so late when she knew at her age he might be orphaned."

Elizabeth bristled at her mother's words but turned away, reaching for her apron on the pantry door. Most times her mother's rantings made no sense, but she always managed to say something nasty about Vera. This was her latest criticism, and she'd mentioned several times in the last while how Vera had left Keefe orphaned, as if she had caused her own death just to spite her sister. Elizabeth knew there was no point even trying to reason with her mother's way of thinking, but it infuriated her nonetheless. It took all her resolve to appear unflustered.

*

"Is she always this bad?" Margaret asked when she returned to the kitchen. "I'm not even sure she knew who I was. She called me Vera twice. 'I know why you are putting me in my room, Vera. You think Tom will ask you to the dance. And I know you took my blue shirtwaist dress right out of my closet. You better bring it back, Vera.'"

"Yes, that's pretty much the way she always is. Some days she's nastier than others. A good day is when she just sits and cries. Those are easier than the days she's in a rage."

"It must be very difficult for you and Father. Does she help out with the house at all? You couldn't leave Keefe alone with her, could you?"

"No, I don't. I am hoping when he starts school I can get a job and possibly make enough money to get a place of our own. For now, I need to be here to look after him. I will make sure he is never again treated the way he was when I was in the hospital."

"I am so sorry I didn't do more then to help out, Elizabeth. I really didn't know how badly he was being treated."

"All water under the bridge now. Let's enjoy your visit. I am anxious to get to know your children, and Keefe will love having other children around."

"You deserve a life, you know. You need to get out and meet people, maybe a man. You'll want to have children of your own eventually."

"I'm fine. I will have my own life someday, but right now all I'm interested in is looking after Keefe. He is my life. Set the table, will you, and then call the children in to wash up for supper. I think I'll take Mother's plate up to her. We'll have a much calmer and quieter meal if she eats in her room."

*

Elizabeth set the birthday cake down in front of Keefe. She struck the match and lit the five candles. Margaret started the children in the singing of "Happy Birthday." Keefe leaned ahead and took a big breath before blowing out all but one candle.

"You won't get your wish," Jason called across the table.

"One more time, buddy. Good boy. Now your wishes will come true," Elizabeth said.

Helen Rogers staggered into the room and the chatter went silent. She leaned on the table and glared at Elizabeth.

"Why is the boy blowing out my birthday candles? I want my birthday cake. Did you think I wouldn't know you gave it to him?" She picked up the plate nearest her and threw it across the table. It bounced off the table, landing on the floor beside Keefe and shattering into several pieces.

Tom Rogers rose to his feet and moved slowly toward his wife. "Calm down, dear. Of course we didn't forget your birthday. Sit down and I'll give you your birthday cake. We were coming up to get you. Light the candles again, Elizabeth, and sing 'Happy Birthday' to your mother."

1962

Margaret Teed hung up the phone and sat staring into the dark room. The only light she could see was the flickering streetlamp as it illuminated the sidewalk outside. Gerald had gone to his Lodge meeting. The children were all asleep; a feat not often achieved this early in the evening.

Her father's words echoed in her head. She was struggling to process the terrible news he had called to tell her: "Your sister is dead. She took her own life."

Father had given no details. She hadn't even asked. Margaret began to sob. Elizabeth had seemed so good when they talked last. She had been so excited about her plan to rent the small house directly across the road from the diner she was working in. "I can have it at the first of next month."

"Don't feel like you have to come, Margaret," her father had said. "You have the children to look after. Your mother is beside herself and isn't up to having any company right now. We will have a small service. Considering the circumstances, I think it's best we just have a private burial. No point in you coming all this way."

"What about Keefe, Father?"

"The boy will miss her for sure, but you've got enough to think about. We'll figure things out, don't you worry. There's lots of folks willing to take him, if we find we can't manage."

Margaret knew how much her sister loved the boy. She could not imagine Elizabeth taking her own life and leaving him. She certainly had seemed like she had overcome the problems that put her in the hospital a few years ago. Perhaps she was much more troubled than she had let on.

Margaret walked into the kitchen and began preparing the children's school lunches for the next day. Could it be the illness that had always gripped her mother had been passed on to her daughters? She'd held on to the belief Elizabeth had overcome her problems and it was this hope that helped when she sometimes suffered the melancholy. She was determined not to end up in any way like the mother she had watched become worse and worse over the years. Perhaps Father was right. There was nothing she could do by coming home now. On the contrary, staying here and protecting her own well-being was the best thing she could do for everyone. Surely it wasn't selfish to put your own children and your own health first.

*

Tom Rogers turned off Gorham's Bluff Road back onto the main road heading for home. The only thing on his mind was a deep feeling of dread about going home. Tonight would be the first night in twenty-some years he would be in the house all by himself. The last two weeks had been unbearable, but at least the boy had been there. The boy hadn't said much, but knowing he was there and had to be looked after gave Tom Rogers reason enough to get up in the morning.

He should be relieved to be going home to a quiet house. He still found himself waking at night with his first thought to go check on Helen. Nights had been the worst in the last few years. Did those nights start before the accident or because of it? It was hard to separate the before and after. Helen had been a care for years, but everything had gotten worse afterwards, and then he'd sent his youngest daughter to a mental hospital.

I sent the wrong one away. The thought hit Tom like a punch and his eyes filled with tears, almost causing him to pull off the road. He had handled everything the wrong way. But surely taking Keefe to the Gorhams' right now was the right thing to do. He was in no state to look after the boy. If only he could muster the courage to call Henry or Margaret. But calling them would force him to face the truth of things, and facing the truth was something he did not feel able to do. At least the boy would be looked after. Don Gorham would work him hard, but Pauline would feed him well, and they won't be mean to the boy. That was a lot more than he could say for the way he and Helen had treated him. And then to take Elizabeth from him. The poor boy was much better off where he was now.

1969

Tom Rogers picked up a pile of newspapers off the cluttered kitchen table. He could not remember the last time he'd set the table for a meal. Usually he stood by the stove, eating something from a pot. Even when the boy was here they seldom sat together for a meal. Last time he just left the food out and let the boy get his and when he was done he would eat whatever was left.

Keefe would be back tomorrow and he had washed the sheets on the bed upstairs and had hung them on the line, even though they would probably freeze solid before drying. The kid probably wasn't too happy about coming back. He couldn't blame him there. What kid would want to live here? Why had he not given the boy a better chance by putting him up for adoption right after Helen passed?

Tom seldom acknowledged the reasons for anything he had done since Helen died. Since long before that day, actually. Possibly since the day the honeymoon came to such an abrupt end when Helen first started getting so hard to deal with. Theirs had been no storybook life, for darn sure. But he would do his best to look after the boy. There was seven cord of firewood to be put in the cellar, which would keep them busy for a few days. And then the kid could get back to school.

Tom remembered how much Henry had loved school since the day he started. It certainly hadn't been the same in his case. Tom had only gone to grade six, then started working in the woods with his father. But Henry even as a young boy had a love of learning.

"I'm going to wear one of those flat hats on my head and a big robe like the minister's when I go to universe." Henry had been so little he hadn't even been able to pronounce the word *university*. He went off to university, all right, even though his father couldn't even spell the word. Henry had always wanted to study about rocks, and he had done just what he set out to do, no credit to anything his father had done to help him. He had not been the father his own kids had needed, and for sure he wasn't likely to do any better with Jud and Vera's boy.

Tom took a swipe at the other clutter on the table, knocking it all into the cardboard box with the newspapers. He set the box beside the basement door and picked up the straw broom and dustpan from the corner. *Oh, I'm Suzy Homemaker today*, Tom thought as he started sweeping the kitchen floor.

PART FOUR
1990–1991

Once Keefe finished the paintings of the house, both interior and exterior, he painted some landscapes depicting the property as he envisioned it before the mudslide. He began with the view from the beach. He used the many sketches of the property he had done as a teenager as a starting point for his interpretations.

"I sat on the beach for hours and sketched this one," Keefe said. "It was February and the ice and snow altered the landscape of course, but I remember imagining it in the summer. I imagined the house still standing and was convinced I would see the roof from the large rock on the shore. Imagine my childhood if I had lived there. I loved the river when I was a kid, but I rarely got there. There was no path to the shore on my uncle's property, but most of the trees had been cut so I was able to see the river from the upstairs hall window."

"You spend every waking hour at the river with the kids when we visit Mom and Dad. You own the property, you know. Someday you could go back and sit on that beach, maybe even build a camp or something."

"I don't know if I'll ever want to build on that property.

Maybe the kids will someday. I don't know, but I do know saying no to the offers I've had in the last few years from people wanting to buy it has been the right thing. I'm not ready to let the property belong to someone else. Not yet, anyway."

"Is this field you've painted still like this, or are you imagining it as it was before the mudslide?"

"The field, when I sketched it, anyway, looked just like this. I expect it's grown up a bit now, though. I think the Fullertons cut hay there when I was a kid. I remember seeing a truck filled with hay come up the driveway one time and remember my uncle swearing, saying they should be paying him for the hay."

"What about the tree?"

"I completely dreamed up that tree. I have no idea if one like it grew in the yard. If it had, it might have been strong enough to withstand the destruction. No, I put this tree in the yard and put a treehouse high in its branches because as kid I dreamed about just such a tree and a place of my very own. Suppose I could have sat in my treehouse and drawn pictures of the sites around me to show my parents. Would they have stuck them to the fridge like you do when the kids bring home their masterpieces? Would Dad have helped me build it? Would the ladder still be there, inviting my own children to climb into my sanctuary?"

"Are you finding all this *what if* kind of thinking as you paint comforting or upsetting? I know I am finding the writing very emotional. I feel so angry and sad about what happened and I can only imagine how it is making you feel. Are we doing the right thing, looking at this so closely?"

"A year ago I would have said for sure we shouldn't be putting ourselves through this needless exercise when the past is over and done with. But now I feel I have been given a lens to see things differently. It is heartbreaking but freeing in some way. All the years I pushed thoughts about my parents as far out of my head as I could, and now I am welcoming the time spent absorbed in thoughts about them. I feel like I have been given a gift of doing what I love to do while at the same time filling the empty places all those years left. I am thankful you pushed me toward it."

"Did I push you, or were you just ready and let whatever I did propel you to a place you have been waiting your whole life to give yourself permission to go? We're in this together, Keefe, and however difficult it is, you have earned the right to feel whatever you feel. And if you want to spend hours pretending you are a boy sitting in a treehouse, you go right ahead."

*

Henry Rogers pulled his SUV onto the site and put it in park. He had been on the Ace Mining site every day this week but had been oblivious to the anxiety he'd been feeling since starting this project. The dream he woke from last night had crystallized what he'd been feeling even before arriving in the Northern Ontario town his firm had sent him to a week ago. He had been sent as a consultant for the mining company.

They were experiencing major erosion problems.

In the dream, he was a boy. Those early days had been pushed so far back in his adult brain it took him awhile to realize as he lay awake trying to process the dream, the place he'd been was Uncle Jud and Aunt Vera's beach. As a boy, he had spent endless hours there, usually by travelling the creek bed across his father's property and onto Uncle Jud's, making his way down to the river's edge. He would take this trek in all seasons, even when the swelling water of the spring freshet made it impossible to navigate the jutting rocks normally providing a footpath down the creek. During the high water, he would zigzag through the thick brush, trying to stay as close to the stream's edge as possible. More than a few times he had gotten a good soaking from walking too close.

Henry had always been obsessed with rocks, the outcroppings and the formation of the ledge underneath. The surface was constantly shifting, especially in the spring or after a heavy rain, and it was always like a treasure hunt for Henry to discover what the earth's moving had revealed.

He'd been sobbing when he woke from the dream. He finally got back to sleep, but he felt a heaviness this morning. He looked over at his briefcase with the imprint "AGA Howe International" embossed on the front. He had done very well professionally and was at the top of his field, but when was the last time he'd felt the thrill that led him to make this his life's work? Was it even a thrill, or had it been the need to prove something to his father?

His father had not been in the dream, which made perfect sense, since his parents never went to Uncle Jud's and Aunt Vera's. But it had been a second home for him, Margaret, and Elizabeth; a sanctuary for him and his sisters. Somehow in the dream there had been a foreboding, a fear his father was going to ruin the beauty of this place.

Two weeks ago, Henry started the research and investigation into the problems Ace Mining was experiencing partly due to a large area being clear-cut by a sister company. Why did people have such difficulty understanding the relationship trees had to the soil? They couldn't see the forest for the trees, so to speak. It had hit him like a blow to the head as he pored over the photographs he had been sent.

He had never actually seen the devastation. He hadn't been home again after Margaret's wedding, and as guilty as he felt about not attending Vera and Jud's funeral, going to see where his aunt and uncle had died was something he could not bring himself to do. It became easier to stay away as the years went by. Even after he and Heather were married and started their family, the only contact with his past was a call to Margaret each Christmastime.

Such destruction. As he stared at the photographs of the Northern Ontario landscape all he could think of was his childhood home; the fields, the hills, the woods, the streambeds, and the beaches he had tramped as a boy. The people he had loved. His beloved aunt and uncle, his dear, sweet sister, Elizabeth. They had died as a result of similar destruction.

The destruction he had not been able to prevent.

*

Keefe pulled the last suitcase from the trunk. Packing for three weeks in New Brunswick was getting more challenging as the kids got older. Convincing Melanie she didn't need to bring everything she owned on the visit was not easy. Zac didn't care so much and had packed his duffel bag so quickly that Summer realized when inspecting it later that he hadn't even packed any underwear or socks.

"I'm mostly going to be in my bathing suit anyway, Mom," Zac explained. "Can we go to the beach Dad painted? I like Nan and Gramps's beach, but I really want to see Dad's beach."

"I think you probably can, but you'll have to ask Dad."

*

Summer walked across the yard toward Keefe. When they had driven in a few minutes ago she had made a beeline for the bathroom, barely greeting her parents.

"You unpacked the trunk fast. Sorry I didn't help you. Not taking you up on your offer to stop in Welsford for a bathroom break was almost disastrous. I thought I was going to burst."

"Mom, we don't need to hear the details," Zac hollered from the steps. "Can we go to the river? Nan said supper wouldn't be ready for about twenty minutes."

"Yes, but don't go in the water until one of us gets there."

"We both know how to swim, Mom," Melanie protested.

"We aren't little kids anymore."

"They aren't little kids," Keefe echoed, reaching out and hugging his wife. "They are growing up so fast. Maybe it's time we have another one."

"I always thought I wanted more kids, but now I'm not so sure. I don't know if I want to go through the whole baby thing again. The kids are so independent now. Would we really want to start all over again?"

"I would, but of course I'm not the one doing most of it."

"Yeah, I'm the one who's a hotel for nine months and a restaurant for nine more. I'll think about it, Mr. Williams. But now let's go look after the two we already have."

*

"I want to go talk to your uncle again while we're here, Keefe," Summer said. The kids and the grandparents had gone to bed and Summer and Keefe were enjoying the late evening on the screened-in back veranda.

"Why would you want to do that?" Keefe replied.

"There's something nagging at me and I just can't put my finger on it. I've fleshed out the story as much as I can with everything Gladys has shared with me, but it feels like I'm missing something."

"What is there to miss? The bastard cut all the trees, heavy rains came, and my parents' lives were washed away in an avalanche of mud."

"When I talked to the two men who worked with him they

gave me a perspective I'd never considered before. I think a lot of what your uncle did, he did because of your aunt. Your uncle said it was time the truth was told."

"Whose truth? He never admitted to anything. She didn't make him cut every tree off the hill. She didn't make him rent me out. She was a nasty woman, but he was the one who ran the show."

"It might seem that way, but I think she had quite a hold on him. Dave Evans said he bent over backwards to make her happy. *Happy* probably isn't even the right word; to keep her calm, to keep her contained. I think your uncle gave in to her and did whatever it took to prevent her angry, sometimes violent, outbursts. I don't know if he will talk to me about it, but I want to try."

"My aunt was mean. It was her I was the most afraid of, but he was every bit as nasty. He never hit me, though, until that last night. The only time I saw a shred of kindness in him was when he dealt with Aunt Helen's outbursts. He always seemed able to quiet her down. He talked to her in a whisper like she was a frightened animal and basically gave her whatever she wanted. But he always seemed as scared of her as I was."

"See, that's what I mean. I think her mental condition and his attempts to manage her led to the choices he made. It must have been terrible dealing with her day after day. When I think of his life I do start to feel sorry for him."

"Really, I can't say I ever felt sorry for him. It used to make me so angry he'd give in to my aunt every time over the least little thing but wouldn't show a bit of kindness to Elizabeth."

"Or you. I know he didn't treat you well and I can completely understand how you feel about him. I am not looking to let him off the hook. I just want to see the whole picture. I think much of what happened, happened because your aunt had a powerful hold over him. He loved his wife and tried to look after her as best he could. She was very unwell. She should have received help for her mental illness, but your uncle dealt with it the only way he knew how."

"Go see him. I don't feel any desire to hear his side of things, but you go right ahead. I have long stopped analysing why my uncle did what he did. I can't imagine anything will change how I feel. But you're the writer. I suppose it will make a better story if you can find a shred of decency in the bad guy."

*

On Summer's second visit to Tom Rogers the condition of the ramshackle house was worse than before. He opened the door after several loud knocks and Summer could see his physical state had deteriorated as well.

"How's that book of yours coming along?" he asked even before Summer spoke.

"How are you doing, Tom?"

"I'm still living."

"Do you think I could come in and talk awhile?"

"Yeah, sure. Don't take your jacket off. It's cold and damp in here. I think the roof's been leaking upstairs, but I haven't got the strength to go up and look. Wouldn't it be a hoot if the house collapsed on me and killed me in my sleep?"

*

"There's two hundred and thirty-four thousand dollars in this account, Summer," Keefe called across the yard to Summer where she had walked away from the veranda, letting Keefe open the envelope addressed to him in privacy.

When Summer came up on the veranda Keefe passed her the bank book and the letter. She sat on the bench across from Keefe and read the short note.

> Keefe, I do not have the right words to say just how sorry I am for everything. I have lived with a terrible guilt and my life has been cursed beyond anything you could imagine. Every day I wish things had been different. I wish you had grown up with your parents and lived the life you were meant to have. Nothing I can say at this point will ever change the tragedy I caused. I am enclosing the bank book for an account I opened in your name the week after your parents died. I know no amount of money could ever compensate for their loss, but I hope in some small way this demonstrates my remorse. Perhaps with this money you will be able to reclaim your parents' property and maybe even build a home and a life to replace the one stolen from you.
>
> Tom Rogers

"Two hundred and thirty-four thousand dollars, Summer. Can you believe he put that much money in an account for me? I am shocked. Part of me feels angry he thinks he can give me money, blood money, for what he did…but a small part of me is totally surprised he cared enough to save this for me. I really don't know what to think."

"I know. But think for a minute what he has had to live with. He lost his wife and a daughter, not to mention the two living children who have nothing to do with him. He has lived with a reputation of causing his sister- and brother-in-law's deaths, and for the most part the community shunned him. What pleasures has he had in his life? He is approaching death and has nothing but misery to show for the life he lived. I think at least by giving you this money he gets some relief from the hell he has lived through. Whether he brought the hell on himself or not doesn't even seem to matter after all this time."

"Do you think we could do what he suggests? I know I have always said I would never live here again, let alone live on the property where my parents died, but do you think we could? It isn't even the money, although God knows it would sure help to have this money sitting in the bank. Do you think we could make a life there? I know your parents would be all for it, and I can't imagine the kids putting up much of a fight."

"I don't know, Keefe. I love the life we have. We built a life and a home where we are. But maybe moving here is the next step. We can both do what we do wherever we live. The kids could adjust to it, I'm sure. It is something to consider. Let's not mention it to the kids or to Mom and Dad just yet. We need to get our heads around it. Once we get back home and I finish the book and you finish getting your exhibit ready we will be in a better state to think about the possibility of moving back here. I want to get Henry's and Margaret's letters to them too. I don't know if whatever he wrote to them will shed any more light on things, but it feels like they might add more to the whole picture."

*

Henry Rogers reread the letter. It had been waiting for him when he returned from his second trip to Northern Ontario. Summer Williams's return address was on the envelope and he couldn't imagine what she would be sending him. When he realized after opening the envelope it contained a letter from his father and some legal documents, he wasn't completely sure he wanted to read it. Heather wouldn't be home until Friday. Maybe he would leave the inner envelope unopened until she got home. He had been messed up enough lately without facing whatever this contained.

Messed up, not sleeping, on edge, and downright weepy. What was wrong with him? Two days ago, he had stood and cried at the site where several acres of ground had shifted. The mine manager and two other colleagues had been taken aback for sure. He wasn't even sure what he'd said to them before rushing to his rental car and making a beeline for his hotel room. If a remote hill in Northern Ontario could bring such emotion, how would he react to whatever this was from his father?

I'm a grown man, for God's sake, Henry admonished himself. *I am not a little boy or a "wet-behind-the-ears, fancy college student."*

Henry,

I'm thinking the last person you expect to get a letter from is me. I am writing it nevertheless. The doctor tells me my heart might conk out anytime. I'm probably already pushing up dandelions by the time you get this letter. I thought about sending it in the mail but I don't have the foggiest idea what your address is. Pretty sad when a father doesn't even know where his own son lives. I take the full blame for that. I don't blame you for not keeping in touch after me telling you I never wanted to see you again. I didn't mean it even as I was saying it.

Try as I might I can't come up with a good excuse for treating you so badly, but there are some things I need to tell you. First of all, as you can see in the will, I am leaving you everything. Years ago, I opened an account and deposited money for your cousin. The rest is yours. Might be nice if you gave Margaret something but it's up to you. I owe you this land. God knows you'll probably want to sell it and be done with this mess. You knew every inch of this land and loved it. What you tried to tell me was dead on. I had blinders on when it came to the damage I was doing.

It's hard to write the words to make you understand it wasn't really greed that drove me and made me do the things I did. I don't want to disrespect your mother or her memory and I am not laying the blame on her. She was not a well woman. I did not handle things the way I should have but I didn't know what else to do. I loved your mother. I don't think she ever believed that and I spent every day trying to convince her I did. By the time I realized exactly what her demon was it was much too late. There was nothing I could have done to make her feel loved. She was troubled, more troubled than any of us knew. She was so full of guilt, anger, and jealousy and was downright nasty especially to your Aunt Vera. She always accused me of settling for her when I couldn't have her sister, which was not true. I never had feelings for Vera but Helen was irrational about that, along with everything else.

Your mother wanted the best of everything and I worked hard to provide but it was never enough. I got so wrapped up in making enough money to satisfy her wants I didn't even see what I was turning into. The hill and those trees was just the tipping point. A tipping point all right. Our already miserable life became a living hell after the hill came down and Vera and Jud were killed.

I wish I had listened to you and stopped the cutting.

If I had made things better with Jud and Vera right then, things would have been a whole lot different. I don't know what the storm would have brought but I would wager a bet it wouldn't have caused the destruction it did if I had stopped the cutting in December when you told me to. I've got the papers, the report they did afterwards and I am sending it to you with the will and this letter. Catastrophic failure, they called it. You'll read the report and you will see it was exactly like you said. I did not listen to my own son and that has been the hardest cross to bear in all this.

*

Two weeks later Summer drove to Margaret's to deliver her letter.

"I can leave the room if you would like to be alone to read your father's letter," Summer said after passing Margaret the envelope.

"If you don't mind I would rather just read it out loud to you. You are as close to all this as I am, if not closer. I have distanced myself from what happened so many years ago. I can't imagine what a letter from my father would even say. You may as well hear it at the same time I do."

Margaret, I was not a good father and I was a worse grandfather. I am sure your children came away from their one visit not caring if they ever saw either grand-parent again. I am sorry. You must have been glad to get away too. If I had been thinking straight, I would have insisted Elizabeth and the boy go with you. God forgive me. If I had done that your sister would still be alive. You must not feel any guilt as you had your own children to think about. I honestly thought I could keep your mother under control. I made excuses for her your whole life but I know now by doing that I made things worse for you all. I should have gotten her the help she needed. I should have put my children first and not tried to pretend I could fix her.

The doctor says I have a heart problem and might not live much longer. I am probably dead by the time you read this and God knows who found this letter. I have lived a sorry excuse for a life. But as I come close to dying I need to set some things straight. First of all, I need to tell you the truth about what happened to Elizabeth. I don't expect you to understand why I chose to lie about the way Elizabeth died. At the time, I thought it was the best for everyone.

Your sister did not kill herself. I don't know if you knew just how violent your mother could get. It got harder and harder to control her but I never thought she would do what she did. The boy was at school. Your sister was working at the diner by the ferry and she was getting ready to leave for work. I was in the barn. It had come to the point we never left your mother alone.

Elizabeth was putting her coat on when your mother descended on her. She was in a rage. If only I had come in a few minutes sooner.

Who would have thought your frail mother would have the strength to do what she did? Your mother took the belt from Elizabeth's coat. She took the belt and strangled your sister. I came in to the last seconds of your sister's struggle. It was as if I were seeing a monster. Your mother was not even aware of what she was doing. God forgive me, I hung a rope from the beam in the summer kitchen and made it look like your sister hung herself. Helen did not seem to realize what she had done. I thought I could cover it up and spare her the shame. She must have known, though, because a week later she swallowed every pill in her bottle and took her own life.

"Oh my God!" Margaret cried. "Poor Elizabeth. Poor, poor Elizabeth. I should have known. I never understood how she could have left the boy. I should have known better. I should have questioned it. My poor, dear sister. How could my mother have done such an evil thing and how could my father just cover it up? Why would he tell me now? It just gives me more of a reason to feel guilty for not doing anything. How could he do this to me?"

Summer took the letter from Margaret's hands and continued reading.

My pride and stubbornness kept me from admitting the truth. I knew I was in no state to raise the boy and it was the week after your mother died I sent him to work on the Gorhams' farm. Over the years it was the only way I could have him looked after without exposing just how desperate I was. Somehow I kept going day by day. It's funny how lies grow into the truth if you say them to yourself often enough.

Summer set the letter down and put her arms around Margaret. "I know this is very difficult for you, but I think he needed to finally let the truth out. Imagine the torture it has been for him all these years. I am not excusing his behaviour. I can't even imagine how he did what he did, but he has suffered for it. He knows he made terrible mistakes all the way along and he has suffered the consequences of every action he took. I am not saying you need to forgive him. I am just trying to explain his need to tell you the truth, as awful as it is for you to hear."

"My poor sister and poor Keefe. At least now he will know Elizabeth didn't leave him on purpose. She loved him as if he were her own. My parents took the lives of his parents and the one person who would have done everything in her power to give him the love he deserved. What does it make me in all this? How could I have been so callous and not stepped in to make it right?"

"You are not to blame, Margaret. You were young, just

trying to find your own way and raise your own family. It is easy to look at the past and clearly see what you should have done, but at the time it is never straightforward. It is complicated. Of course you have regrets, but what happened is not your fault. The past cannot be changed. It has unfolded as it has and there is no point torturing yourself about it. If it makes you feel any better, I am thankful you didn't take Keefe, or I never would have met him."

Margaret released herself from Summer's embrace and walked across the room. She stood staring out the window as Summer continued speaking.

"We are where we are right now and we have to move on from here. Your father set aside money for Keefe all these years. He started an account for him a week after your aunt and uncle died. He has given this money to Keefe and it is a large amount. We are considering moving back to the peninsula and building a home on Vera and Jud's property. Maybe at last some real healing will take place and our two families can come back together. I'm sure it's what your aunt and uncle would have wanted. Maybe your kids and grandkids can finally have a chance to enjoy the places you loved as a kid."

"Maybe," Margaret replied weakly.

*

"This is the final painting," Keefe stated as he led Summer into his studio. "Zac will like it the best I'm sure, with his obsession for heavy machinery."

"He'll probably know it is Bill Palmer's excavator, but he won't know what this painting really signifies for us. When will we tell the kids our plans?"

"I want to get this exhibit over with. Then I think we should put the house up for sale. Suppose your parents would mind if we live with them for a bit while the house is getting built?"

"Are you kidding? Mom is going to be completely behind this move. She will be so happy to have her grandchildren nearby. Do you know how hard it's been not to tell her about our decision? And it's been so hard to keep our other news from her. She will be able to guess as soon as she sees you when they come for the exhibit next week."

"It's so hard not to blurt out both things every time I talk to her on the phone."

"We will tell them as soon as they get here next week. I will want to go down and stay with them when Bill Palmer starts working on the property. He says he can start as soon as the frost is out if it's not a wet spring. We'll both want to go to New Brunswick when Tony Henderson finishes the plans for the house. We need to decide where exactly to build it."

"I think it's so neat, that the son of the man who did the plans for your parents' house is doing our plans and building our house. These next few months are going to be crazy busy but unbelievably exciting, especially since I've stopped throwing up."

*

The fact they were moving to New Brunswick and building a house was not kept a secret from the kids until after the exhibit, though, because Melanie happened to need a drink of water the night her grandparents arrived. The deep conversation Summer and Keefe were having with Don and Marilyn Barkley after the kids had gone to bed was what Melanie overheard when she came in to the kitchen.

"We're moving to New Brunswick?" Melanie cried out excitedly. "When? Can I go tell Zac? He's not sleeping. He has his tape player on listening to stupid Milli Vanilli's 'Blame It On the Rain' song over and over again."

"That's very ironic, don't you think?" Don Barkley said.

"Go get your brother, Melanie. Dad and I might as well tell you both exactly what is going on."

"We already figured out you're having a baby, Mom. We're not little kids."

"So the first step is to get the property cleaned up," Keefe continued explaining to Marilyn and Don. "Bill Palmer assures me he can do the work to reshape the ground around where the house stood."

"I have no doubt Bill Palmer can do it if anyone can," Don replied. "I wish it had been as easy to clean up the disastrous spill from the *Exxon Valdez*. Can you believe it, 11.3 million gallons of oil? What is wrong with people? No regard for the environment. At least back when your uncle caused his destruction people didn't know any better. We are supposed to be more enlightened these days. It's the nineties, for God's sake."

"You've got him all riled up now," Marilyn Barkley said.

"What is Melanie talking about? She said we're moving to New Brunswick," Zac said, coming into the kitchen. "Can I have some chips?"

"Yes, grab some chips and sit down, son. Mom and I have a lot to tell you."

*

It had been no coincidence the gallery had chosen Keefe's thirty-seventh birthday for the exhibit. When mulling over the possible dates, the significance of presenting paintings to honour the life and loss of Vera and Jud Williams on the date their cherished son had been born seemed clear to Summer and Keefe.

"It's going to be hard enough to publicly display paintings with such deep meaning to me, so it being my birthday won't make any difference. You won't have to plan a surprise party for me, anyway."

Keefe fastened the pearl buttons on the cuffs of his white shirt. With a bit of convincing he had agreed to wear a tuxedo to the exhibit. He reached into the closet for the jacket, turning to look at Summer as she sat putting the finishing touches on her makeup.

"Remember the cake your mom made me the first year I lived with you guys? That was my best birthday ever. And the best birthday present I ever got was having you and your parents believe in me. I never thought I would be so thrilled to be moving back home. I can't wait until this night is over and all the hype my agent has created around the exhibit has passed. When it's done, we can concentrate on getting our new home and our new life underway."

"I'm very proud of you, Keefe."

"I'm pretty proud of you too, Summer Barkley Williams. None of this would be happening if you hadn't seen me way back then. Have to say, I'm even glad Winston Rideout threw me out of the boys' bathroom and got your attention."

"I think I'll use the name of your exhibit as the title for my book, if it's all right with you," Summer said. "*When the Hill Came Down* seems fitting for both, I think."

"It's too bad Gladys Titus couldn't be here tonight," Keefe said. "She really had so much to do with the paintings and your book."

"I know. I'm going to send her some pictures. Maybe your paintings will get shown in Saint John after we get settled, or even in the museum they are putting in the basement of Macdonald Consolidated, and she can see them then. Can you believe the dungeon-like classrooms down there are being converted into a museum? Where more fitting for your paintings to be shown than on the peninsula and in that school?"

"Right now I have to muster up my courage to get through this night. Sometimes I wish I could attend these things in disguise. I would much rather hear what people think when they're not just sucking up to the artist. Some honest comments from people who really take the time to look at the paintings would be so nice to hear."

"Oh stop, you will hear some sincere comments. You have put your heart and soul into this work and each painting is a masterpiece as far as I'm concerned."

"See what I mean? Sucking up to the artist. Let's go, Mrs. Williams. I can do this with you by my side."

*

Summer knew who the man she spotted across the room must be. He did look a bit like his father, but it was his demeanour and his expression when he turned away from the painting entitled "The Torrent" that made her certain the man was Henry Rogers. The emotion she saw on his face was personal and deep and she quickly walked to greet him.

"Henry?" Summer asked.

"Yes. You must be Summer."

"Keefe will be so pleased you came."

"I don't mean to intrude. Your husband's work is amazing. They're hard to look at, though."

"You are not intruding. It's a public exhibit, of course, but I know for you it is much more. This story is as much yours as it is ours. You have never even met your cousin, have you? Come with me and I'll introduce you two. It is about time you got to know each other. Margaret and Gerald are here too with Jason and Meredith. I hope you can stay for the reception afterwards. Did you come alone?"

"Yes, I came by myself. I would love to meet Keefe if he

has the time to speak with me. We have a bit of catching up to do, I think."

Summer walked to the podium. She looked out at the crowd before looking directly at Keefe, who stood a few feet away looking more like he would rather be at home watching tonight's episode of *Law and Order* than mingling with the throng of people in attendance.

She began: "My husband and I would like to thank everyone so much for coming. First of all, to my parents, Don and Marilyn Barkley, who are here from New Brunswick for this special night, we say a big thank you for all your love and support over the years. Thanks to our two kids, Zachary and Melanie. You guys are the best. We are so pleased that my husband's cousins Henry Rogers and Margaret and Gerald Teed and their children Jason and Meredith could be with us tonight as well.

"A big thank you to the Rosemount Gallery and Thomas and Evelyn Robinson. Thank you to my husband's agent, Evan Dryer. They have all worked tirelessly to make this evening a wonderful success.

"I met Keefe Williams when he was fifteen years old. On one of our first meetings he took a folded scrap of paper from his jeans pocket and passed it to me. At that very moment I knew Keefe Williams was an artist. My husband has already had much acclaim. He has won awards and his paintings hang in homes and in public places. One of his paintings hangs in the Ontario Legislature. My husband has accomplished much in a relatively short career.

"But the exhibit he presents to you tonight is by far his greatest achievement.

"My husband was an infant when he lost his parents in a tragedy more fitting for a movie script than real life. My husband lived his early years in the shadow of that tragedy. Keefe's art lay dormant but found its way to the surface, shedding a light bright and piercing enough to illuminate the darkness.

"It is our hope tonight that as you look at these paintings you will see more than destruction and loss. This series represents the lives of Vera and Jud Williams. It tells their story, a story of dreaming, of planning, of building, of loving and believing. It also tells how that life was destroyed and what was stolen from the infant boy who survived.

"As my husband's talent emerged, I believe these paintings were waiting to be created. This series is by far the masterpiece of a young boy who survived to become the man he is today. I hope when you take the time to look at these paintings, you will see and celebrate in your own lives the power we have as humans to overcome terrible loss, to find strength and resilience and to look for the hope that keeps us going. Please enjoy the evening."

*

Two weeks later, Keefe and Henry met up at the Toronto airport. From their long talk after the exhibit and three follow-up visits, it was as if the two men had known each other their whole lives. When Henry heard Keefe was planning to stay at his in-laws for a few days while Bill Palmer started the excavation work on the property, he offered to make the trip to New Brunswick with him.

"It is so good of Don and Marilyn to let me stay with them. I certainly wouldn't want to stay with my father, but I could have stayed in Saint John somewhere."

"Don't be ridiculous, Henry. They don't mind at all. In fact, they are thrilled you're coming with me. You will have to put up with Don's questions, though. He has a real interest in geology and considers himself quite an expert on the environment. He'll be right there looking over our shoulders. Do you think you will go see your father while we're there?"

"I haven't decided," Henry replied. "I'm not sure what the point of going to see him would be, but since getting his letter I have started to consider the possibility of getting in touch with him. I'll see when I get there. A lot of years have gone by. I suppose I really should make an effort to see him at least once before I come for his funeral and to clean things up. He is leaving me everything, you know, but I have already told Margaret she gets half of whatever the place brings."

"You don't think you will ever live there or maybe use it for a summer place? And what about your kids?"

"I guess I should never say never. Look at you. I bet you never thought you would be building on your parents' property."

"No, I did not. When I left the peninsula I was certain it was the last place I ever wanted to live. Funny how things change."

*

Keefe and Henry sat with Don Barkley at his kitchen table. Marilyn had prepared a feast to welcome them. Now the table had been cleared off, and Henry set down the document he had briefly mentioned while they were eating.

"This is the geological report my father sent me. It is pretty simple compared to the investigation they'd carry out if something similar were to happen nowadays."

"God forbid it would happen these days," Don said. "Surely we know better, although I sometimes wonder if Irving really considers the environment when they cut a block of wood. Luckily most land on the peninsula is privately owned and the old guys know what they're doing. Stan Whelpley has more wisdom than anyone who's been to university, as far as I'm concerned."

"I won't take that as an insult, Don. I believe the old farmers and woods workers know a lot for sure. They might not know the technical stuff, but they have the common sense. Unfortunately, common sense didn't come into it at all when Dad was cutting trees. Have a look at this report. It tells you all about your land too, Keefe, which should help you figure out just what you want Bill Palmer to do and just where you might want to build the house. Lots of ledge in the area. Clay on shale. It was the perfect storm causing the hill to come down. Layers of clay had been held in place for hundreds of years through all types of weather because indigenous tree varieties had taken root in the shallow earth."

Keefe picked up the report. It was dated August 19, 1954. After scanning the page, he began reading the introduction out loud.

> This report was commissioned by the Department of Natural Resources and was carried out by the Geological Engineering Department, University of New Brunswick. The seconded professionals and their qualifications are stated in Appendix 1. This analysis was requested after a serious landslide on the parcel of land identified in the section entitled Land Description. The topography of the aforementioned parcel is detailed in the Maps and Diagrams section. An anecdotal explanation of factors leading to the compromise of the escarpment is detailed in the section entitled Background. The last section entitled Conclusion offers the findings of the professionals tasked with determining the factors causing the severe deterioration of the escarpment in question.

Keefe set the paper down. "It's so technical, so clinical, not a snippet of any feeling or compassion for the lives lost when the escarpment was *compromised*. Not sure I can look at the rest of it. All I can picture are men in suits with clipboards tramping around the ruins of my parents' dreams. Pretty sure whatever I read in this report won't change anything. And what was the point of even investigating it? No charges were laid and no blame given to the one person everyone knows was responsible. And to think he got a copy. Who would have paid for the investigation, even though it wouldn't change a damn thing? Did you know at the time it was being investigated?"

"I was just an undergrad. I had no idea the university was asked to do this report. It does make sense though. It was a major landslide and I am sure their research became a teaching tool and was probably responsible for policy recommendations regarding clearcutting."

"That's something you can be pleased about, Keefe," Don said. "I know it doesn't make anything easier, but at least your parents' deaths weren't totally in vain."

"Yeah, I suppose. I would feel better if they had pointed a finger directly at my uncle, though."

"I think he got the message, whether his name was put in the conclusion paragraph or not," Henry said. "The fact he sent me the report along with his letter was an attempt to offer an apology. I believe he has accepted the blame all these years, whether his behaviour reflected it or not."

"I suppose like you said having a topographical map does come in handy for Bill to see. I only want the base of the hill excavated, though. I want what remains of the house to be covered over, but I want the hill left the way it is. I want nature to be the only change the hill ever sees. I want to put a garden where the house was. A garden of roses and shrubs and lots of flowers, a maze of paths, and I want to build a stone wall and put benches and a water fountain, maybe. I want the kids to remember their grandparents and I want something beautiful to replace the destruction. I guess I don't own the hill anyway. I hope you agree with me, since it will be yours soon."

"Absolutely. As long as I'm alive the hill will be untouched," Henry said.

"A garden sounds perfect, Keefe," Don said. "Just perfect."

"Where do you think you'll build the house?" Henry asked.

"Closer to the river, I think. Bill Henderson still had the plans for the house Mom and Dad built. Tony sent a copy to us and we want to build ours to look like the original one, with only a few changes. Summer wants a large sunroom attached, part of it for my studio and the other part for her office. I just hope I can afford to keep painting after we build it. I might apply to Macdonald Consolidated. They are looking for a part-time art teacher. Something about returning as a teacher appeals to me, not to mention a steady income would be nice. Summer has put so much time into writing my story she hasn't had a money maker lately."

"Your in-laws can help out if you need us," Don interjected. "Marilyn will supply you with fresh vegetables and preserves. She gardens like she has to feed a small village."

"I'm sure we'll manage, Don. The money Tom gave me is making this possible, and if the house sells quickly we should be fine. Tony is coming tomorrow to discuss the plans for building. He figures he can get us in by mid-fall, before Christmas at the latest. Maybe tomorrow morning before he comes we can walk around the property and you can advise me exactly where I should tell him to put the foundation, Henry. You should come with us too, Don. I would appreciate your input."

"Sounds good," Henry replied. "I'm thinking I might stop in and see my father afterwards. I may as well get it over with. I don't suppose you want to come with me, Keefe."

"No, I'll pass on that," Keefe answered.

"I won't be able to go tomorrow morning," Don said. "I have a doctor's appointment. Two downsides to getting old are doctor's appointments and funerals. We seem to have a lot of both."

*

Tony Henderson pulled up in his blue half-ton shortly after Keefe and Henry got to the property. Keefe walked toward Tony and the other man getting out of the passenger side.

"Pleased to finally meet you," Keefe said, extending his hand to Tony. "I feel from our correspondence I already know you, even though you were older than me and I don't remember you from school."

"Yes, good to meet you too. This is Paul Cassidy, my partner. Does he look familiar to you? He says you two were in grade five together."

"Cassidy. Oh yeah. I thought I recognized you. Debbie's your sister, right? She and my wife were friends."

"Yeah. Debbie's my younger sister. I think you were in my older sister Connie's class too."

"Oh, I had more classmates than the average guy, which is what happens when they keep you back every other year."

"Yeah, I know," Paul said. "My brother-in-law quit school at the end of grade nine. He was twenty-one. A shame, really, 'cause you wouldn't find anyone smarter than him in some things. He's the best finish carpenter around. We get him to do the finish work in all our houses. I think you know him—Winston Rideout. He married Debbie."

Keefe knew the expression on his face had changed. He thought he had faced all his apprehension about moving back here. He had spent months while working on the paintings for *When the Hill Came Down* exorcizing his demons. But the mention of Winston Rideout made him feel like he was fifteen again. Could he really live in this place without being thrown back into a mire of insecurity and misery? Shit. He was a grown man.

"Winston's not a bad guy," Paul continued. "I told him we were building a house for you. He said you probably won't want him working on it. He's kind of worried about the book your wife is writing. Debbie heard she's writing about what happened to you. Winston says he doesn't want his kids to know what a Neanderthal he was. He had a rough time of it, you know. I'm not making excuses for him. God knows you had a bad time of it yourself. But Winston's not a bad guy. We can talk about him doing the finish work later. We have a lot to discuss before you have to decide."

"Have you figured out where you want to put the house?" Tony Henderson asked.

"Yes, Henry and I had a good look and have chosen a good spot for it. This is my cousin, Henry Rogers, Tom's son," Keefe said. "Let's go have a look."

Henry, Keefe, Tony, and Paul spent about an hour discussing the foundation placement and the work Bill Palmer would have to do to prepare the site for construction. Henry left the three men discussing the final arrangements, dismissing himself from the conversation.

"I'm going to walk over to see my father," he announced. "I'm going to try to walk along the stream and up to the house. The water is still quite high and it's grown up a lot, but I think I can get through. If I'm not back when you're done, Keefe, do you mind driving over to pick me up? Just honk the horn and I'll come out. You don't have to come in to get me."

He was surprised at just how familiar the first part of the trek felt. It was almost as if the curve of the brook had been etched into his brain. He stopped and looked at the large rock across from where he stood. All the changes and heavy growth, but this large rock still the very same as it had been years ago when he tramped through this path. Perhaps the constancy of rocks was why he had become a geologist. Rocks did not change except for the gradual change hundreds of years could bring. Rocks stayed firmly placed and you could count on their stability.

Tears streamed down Henry's cheeks. Had he known this even as a small boy? Had he been aware his mother's health was so unstable and his father's attempt to manage it kept everything in a state of uncertainty? As a husband and father, Henry could not even imagine the challenge it had been for his father. The physical act of fighting his way through the heavy growth on the banks of this stream and reaching the clearing that held his childhood home was exactly what he needed to do today to finally decide he had to offer the words of forgiveness which had been forming in his brain for weeks.

Henry stood at the edge of the clearing for several minutes. The house looked so weathered and worn. The outbuildings were in varying stages of falling down. He walked toward the front door unsure the rickety steps would bear his weight. Tom Rogers answered Henry's fourth knock. Henry reached out and wrapped his arms around the stooped and shaking shoulders of the old man standing silently in the doorway.

*

After Henry's initial visit to his father he went back every day during the time he and Keefe were in New Brunswick. When they got back to Ontario, Henry spent a long time in Summer's office telling her the details of those meetings.

"During my third visit he really seemed to open up. I told him I would arrive shortly after lunch and visit with him for the afternoon if he was up for it. He was on the veranda when I drove your dad's car in the driveway. He seemed to have been waiting for the chance to unload and he quickly began talking as soon as we went into the house.

"'I know everyone thinks I never gave them a second thought' is how he began," Henry told Summer. "Then Dad blurted out his confession as if he could not contain it any longer."

Tom had said to Henry, "I had been to the barn. The power was out most of the day and I'd come out to check on the one cow I still had at the time. I'd let most of the herd go by then, since my time had become so taken up with lumbering and looking after your mother. It was late. Your mother and sister were asleep, but I had not been able to settle. I had a feeling of foreboding. An uneasy feeling. It was still storming and I kept thinking of Vera and Jud over there with a new baby. I had seen earlier how bad things were washing out and I felt like I should be going over to check on them. I extinguished the lantern and shut the barn door, having decided I would drive over and see how things were, maybe offer to bring them here for a day or two. I wasn't even sure I would be able to get the truck down their driveway. I hated the thought they might be cut off for days.

"As I left the barn I could hear a roar. I thought at the time it must be thunder. The rain was still heavy and I ran to the truck. I slid into the driver's seat and had I not looked toward the house I would have missed her. Your mother was coming down the veranda steps. She was wearing only her thin nightdress and she was already drenched. Even with the howling wind I could hear her screaming. I rushed to her and picked her up in my arms. She was frantic and I could barely make out the words she was screaming at me. She continued her hollering as I carried her into the dark house.

"'You love Vera, not me. Vera is the lovable one. You wouldn't even look at me. You looked when I unbuttoned my dress though. You looked at me as if I were a beast, a hideous beast. If you hadn't pushed me away the boat wouldn't have tipped. It was your fault. It was all your fault. And Vera's fault.'

"She was hysterical and I had no idea what she was talking about until her voice quieted and she whispered a pleading cry with a haunting desperation: 'Austin, Austin, Austin.'

"Your mother was in the rowboat with Austin Mitchell."

"Who was Austin Mitchell?" Henry asked Summer, trying to make sense of what his father had told him.

"He was a young man your Aunt Vera was in love with when she was in her teens. He drowned. Vera was to meet him the day he drowned, but she missed the boat ride across the river. Helen had gone across to the rally but denied seeing Austin that day. She certainly never admitted to knowing anything about the accident. His body wasn't found until weeks later. Just recently Gladys recalled the reason Vera missed the scow. Helen had told Vera a call had come saying the boat was leaving a half hour later than previously arranged. Gladys always thought it was strange Helen had gone to the wharf at the right time, but no one ever considered that Helen might have lied intentionally."

"What a terrible woman my mother was. How could she have been so evil?"

"I am not going to try to answer that. What probably started as unhealthy rivalry and sibling jealousy turned into something much more destructive once Helen made the choice to bury any responsibility for a young man's death and her sister's heartbreak. Her choice altered the course of a lot of lives. Did your father say anything else?"

"Yes," said Henry.

Tom had continued to his son: "I stripped her of her wet nightdress and held her tightly, assuring her that she was all right, that I loved her and wasn't leaving her side. When she finally realized it was me I carried her upstairs. I put a dry nightdress on her and tucked her into her bed. She was crying quietly by then, begging me not to go. I took off my wet clothes and settled in beside her. It was a long time before she drifted off to sleep. I didn't dare disturb her, as I was afraid she would sense my absence if I got up, left the house, and went next door. I stayed perfectly still and eventually I fell into a deep sleep. I heard nothing until Dave Evans woke me with his loud knocking the next morning.

"Later I realized the loud roar I'd heard was the hill coming down. If I had left right away I may have been able to get them out. Turning my head for a split second might have made all the difference.

"Helen kept that secret all those years, never facing the blame she held or telling anyone the truth. Her guilt was her undoing, perhaps the underlying cause of her mental illness. All Helen's jealousy and nastiness were just a mask she hid behind. The hill came down that fateful night, but one action by a girl jealous of her younger sister was the beginning of all the destruction. That is the story."

*

Summer looked out the window of her office at the real-estate sign on the front lawn. The "sold" sign had been added two days ago, but it still hadn't quite registered they were leaving this house. She had brought her babies home to this house. She loved the view, the neighbours, and the life she and Keefe had built here. The task of packing up and leaving seemed daunting and was causing her to question the choice to move back to the peninsula.

The final edits were complete and the book had gone to the printer. It was hard letting it go, but she knew she had done all she could to tell the story as truthfully as possible. It had surprised her how little of Keefe's childhood had made the final draft. It was there, of course, but the pivotal events that happened long before Keefe was even born held the core of the story. She'd finished the book with a scene she imagined from the evening she met Keefe at the bridge. It seemed that scene especially with how everything was unfolding was the full-circle moment needed to end the book.

Keefe watched Summer Williams as she biked to the top of the hill. He sat down on the cement rail of the bridge, pulling his pencil and an empty piece of paper from his pocket. He began sketching the sunset. He could not portray the crimson and the orange hues that created the sky's magnificent beauty. For now, he could only imagine it as he drew the pencil lines.

Keefe folded the paper and put it in his shirt pocket. He slipped the pencil stub into his pants pocket but didn't release his grip. He stood up and began walking up the hill on his way back to the Smiths'. Tonight's drawing showed only shades of grey and not the colours of the sky above him in all its vibrancy. He would remember it, though, just as it looked tonight, and someday he would recreate its splendour. Then the sky would come alive. He held the promise of that transformation in his fingers, in his mind, and most of all deep within his being.

Two more weeks and the kids would be done school and they would load the moving van and head to New Brunswick. Tony and Paul had the foundation in and had already began framing up the house. They had assured Keefe if all went well they could have them in the house by the end of the summer. Staying at Mom and Dad's would seem like a regular summer vacation, other than the fact that all their worldly possessions would be squeezed into the garage.

Zac and Melanie were so excited. They would miss their

friends, but for the most part they were totally looking forward to being close to their grandparents and going to the same school their parents had attended. The same school where their father would be teaching art three days a week starting in September.

"Are you sure this is what you want?" Summer had asked Keefe when he got the letter saying District 19 school board was offering him the job as art teacher at Macdonald Consolidated.

"'The board has reviewed your qualifications and are pleased to offer you the position. We are very pleased to have an artist of your distinction willing to share his talents and expertise with the students of Macdonald Consolidated. We only wish the salary was more in keeping with your worth as an artist.' Isn't that a riot?" Keefe had said when reading the letter. "My worth has increased somewhat from when I was a student. I wonder if any of my teachers are still there. If so, it will be interesting to see if they hold the same opinion."

*

Gladys Titus pulled herself to her feet and walked slowly across the kitchen to the stove. Her joints were aching today and every move she made spoke loudly of her age. Some days she still felt like she had when she was a young bride, but lately those days were few and far between. She was definitely not a young bride. Weldon had been gone for twenty-two years. How had the years gone by so quickly?

Gladys sometimes found herself feeling sorry for her present state but then remembered Vera and how short her life had been and how abruptly it had been taken. Gladys knew she had so much to be thankful for. Her five children all lived nearby and had blessed her with twenty-five grandchildren and seven great-grandchildren. She still lived in her own home and enjoyed good health considering her age.

Summer Williams had asked her so many questions in these last few months and she found herself travelling to the past more and more. So many recollections surfaced as she tried to fill in details about the years before and after the tragedy. How had she forgotten so much? They had all just gone on with their lives. Of course she missed her dear friend, but for the most part, her life had continued as usual.

It had been so hard going to Helen and Tom's that morning, knowing she had to tell Elizabeth the devastating news. Then she and Elizabeth had gone to get the baby, the poor, sweet baby. He had been lying in an apple basket in Ethel Whelpley's kitchen, seemingly unaffected by the terrible events of the night before. But the years following were awful for the boy. Why had she not done more? The excuses she had offered at the time now seemed so feeble. Of course she had been busy with her own family, but Vera would not have let anything stand in her way if it had been Gladys's children left orphaned.

It had been difficult dealing with Tom and Helen Rogers, but she should have been more motivated to intercede, not used that as a reason to leave the situation alone. She was

Vera's best friend, so she of all people should have taken Keefe's well-being the most seriously. The rest of the community stepped back and did not question the happenings under the Rogers's' roof even when poor Elizabeth was hospitalized; they were ready to gossip but not willing to interfere. Gladys had pretended she was different, but besides the occasional kind word to the boy when she saw him, what had she done to support Vera's son?

Everyone knew Helen Rogers was not a well woman, but no one considered it their business. And why had no one ever considered that Helen knew more about Austin Mitchell's drowning than she let on? Vera had been too upset afterwards to connect the dots, but Gladys felt at the time that Helen had lied on purpose so that Vera would miss the outing. Gladys always suspected Helen planned it so she could come between her sister and Austin.

And that's exactly what she tried to do. No doubt she made up some lie convincing Austin to take the rowboat. And the poor guy couldn't even swim. When the boat capsized, Helen must have swum to Caton's Island, dried off, and joined the activities, never letting on that anything happened even when the search for Austin Mitchell began. And the way Helen acted a year later, all holy and religious, followed by a nervous breakdown. Gladys should have known something was up then. All water under the bridge now, though. And not a thing could be done to change any of it. But still it made her blood boil thinking how miserable Helen was to Vera.

Now Keefe and Summer were moving back. Bill Henderson's son was building them a new home on Vera and Jud's property. Gladys had driven down to have a look at the progress the other day. It had taken a lot more out of her than she expected it would. Thirty-seven years had gone by, but driving down the driveway brought it all back.

Gladys had gone to Vera's a week before the terrible night. Vera had made her some turkey soup because Barb's little one had a bad cold. Gladys only dropped in for a few minutes to pick up the soup, wanting to hurry back to help Barb as she had had several sleepless nights. She'd sat for a few minutes holding that precious boy. The week following saw the cold and fever spread through the entire family and Gladys had not even had time to talk to Vera on the telephone. And the weather had been so bad, heavy rain for days on end.

Gladys remembered weeks later crying while holding the pot Vera had sent the soup home in, mourning the friend she would never return the pot to. Gladys never used the pot but stuck it far back in the cupboard. The heavy aluminum pot with its red enamel lid caused a catch in her throat to this day when she looked at it. A few years ago, when Beth was cleaning out the cupboards she suggested her mother throw the pot out, but Gladys had told her to put it back where it belonged.

The house was going to be lovely. It was closer to the river than Vera and Jud's was but seemed to be similar in style. She had been there just about every day when Jud and Vera were building, toward the end anyway. Weldon helped some and

Gladys always tried to contribute some cooking to help Vera feed the crew of men.

Least I can do is make a little something for Summer today, Gladys thought. *I used to feed a houseful but these days I'm lucky if I boil myself a potato. I'll make her a casserole and biscuits. Surely I can muster up the energy.*

*

"Seems like I'll be giving birth twice this month," Summer said to her mother as she opened the envelope Don Barkley had just brought down from the mailbox. "Launching a new book feels like having a baby in some ways. Not as painful, mind you, but just as frightening and exciting. My publisher says I should have the first copies by the end of the month. Almost the same due date as this active little one who seems quite anxious to see the light of day."

"I love the cover choice," Marilyn Barkley said. "It is a beautiful book and you should be very proud of it. Can't wait to see what the other baby will look like. Any feelings about what it's going to be?"

"I think it's a boy. Not sure why, but I just feel like it is a boy. We haven't chosen a name yet either way."

Without warning a deluge of tears erupted. Summer turned away from her mother.

"It's an emotional time for you," Marilyn said, reaching to hug her daughter.

"I'm so sorry, Mom."

"Sorry for what?"

"I get all caught up in stuff and sometimes I forget how hard it must be for you. But you never let on. Zachary reminds me so much of Hudson. I cannot imagine what I would do if anything happened to him. And now I am ready to have another baby and I feel like crying all the time but you just keep on going and give all of us everything you've got. I am so sorry."

"Listen, you have nothing to be sorry for. What happened to your brother was nobody's fault. Millions of choices are made every day and millions of circumstances determine our lives and we have so little control over any of it. I have been blessed with so much. Your father and I were able to keep going and you, Keefe, and soon three grandchildren help us to do that every day. I don't know a lot, but I know this: the control we do have in this life is to be grateful and willing to accept the joy we are given. We have to allow joy to accompany the sorrow or the sorrow becomes too much to handle. You have always been part of the joy and for that you should not feel guilty."

*

From an upstairs window Keefe watched Winston Rideout drive into the yard. After a lot of discussion, he and Summer had agreed to Paul's suggestion and hired Winston do the inside trim work. Even though Keefe had no reservations about the work Winston would do, he had not been looking

forward to their first meeting. He felt awkward to say the
least as he headed out to meet him.

"Keefe, long time no see," Winston said, greeting him with
an outstretched hand.

"Yeah, about sixteen years to be exact."

"Must say, I was surprised when Paul said you wanted me
to do this job. Can't say I'd blame you if you didn't."

"They say you're the best around."

"Found something I could do."

"Yeah, me too."

"An artist, right?"

"Yeah."

"Listen, I want to say right up front, I was an asshole, a real
jerk back when we were in school. Made a sport out of giving
you a hard time. Can't believe how mean I was."

"Yeah, I'd like to say I don't remember, but the truth of it is
you're definitely the one who comes to my mind when I think
of how much I hated school. Wasn't the greatest experience
for me. I was more than happy to get out of there. Did you
hear I'm going back as the art teacher?"

"Yeah, Deb told me. The school's lucky to have you. I hear
you got pretty famous in Ontario. My kids go to MCS. We've
got four. How many you and Summer got?"

"We've got two and one on the way. She's due this month.
Hope to get in the house pretty soon, so it's great things are
ready for you to do the trim work."

"Listen, I want to say I'm sorry for the way I was. At first when I heard Summer was writing about things I was worried about how she was going to make me look. I didn't want my kids to know what an idiot I was in school. My boys have trouble with stuff same as I did but things are a lot different for them. The teachers up there are a lot better than when we were in school. They've got a name for what me and my boys got. Dyslexia. Trouble reading and writing. Back in my day it was just called stupid. Funny ain't it, though I can understand if you don't find it funny. I spent so much time calling you stupid and picking on you so I could cover up how stupid I felt. I never knew there was a reason for the trouble I had. I went back to school and got my GED, graduated from high school four years ago. Better late than never, right? My boys are good kids. Probably more Debbie's doing than mine, but they are kind and thoughtful.

"I've told them what I was like. Wanted to be up front with them so anything they hear about me won't come as a surprise. Hope we can put the past behind us. Real nice house you're building here, Keefe. I think it's great you've moved back. Don't expect we'll be best friends or anything, but I hope you'll accept my apology."

"Maybe our kids will be friends. Figure it's as good a place as any to start to put the past behind us. I think our wives have already taken up where they left off. Who knows about us?"

"Well, glad that's out of the way. I'll get started at what I'm here for. I'll just get my tools out of the truck. Paul said the wood was delivered yesterday. Let's get at it so you can bring the new baby home to a finished house."

*

"Knew before I got here I had a job ahead of me," Heather Rogers said as she and Summer sat on the Barkley's beach watching Zac and Melanie swimming. "I don't think the house has had a good cleaning in at least twenty years. We have concentrated on the downstairs. We brought Tom's bed down and set it up in the dining room. He's just been sleeping on the couch for a long time. He's getting weak. He's winded just crossing the room. Henry told Margaret if she wants to see him alive she should come down soon."

"The last I spoke to her she had no intention of coming down to see him," Summer said. "Has she changed her mind? I think she is still very hurt and angry."

"I know. I can't blame her. What a shock to learn after all these years your own mother strangled your sister and your father covered it up. I was surprised Henry forgave him as readily as he did, but he can't seem to convince his sister their father has suffered enough for his actions. Henry should be here soon. He was just loading the truck for the dump when I left. He was going to stop by and see if Keefe had anything at the house to go. Can you believe you'll be moving in in a few days? Do you think the baby will wait?"

"I went about ten days over for the other two, so we'll probably be all moved in before this one decides to make its entrance."

"I'm sure you're anxious for it to be over with. Such a hot month to be nine months pregnant. I had two of mine in the fall, so I know what it's like."

*

Henry Rogers pulled the metal box out from under the bed. He hadn't noticed it yesterday when he and Heather went through the entire room throwing away the clutter. It wasn't until he moved the mattress off the frame a few minutes ago that he saw the familiar tin box. Even before opening the lid he knew exactly what he would see inside. On the inside lid would be the etched name of the little boy who the contents had once belonged to, Judson Williams, and the box would contain a colourful jumble of metal miniature cars and trucks.

Henry had played with those vehicles for hours at his grandparents' house. He remembered the day Aunt Vera let him take them home with him. He had carried the box home proudly but had quickly hidden them in his bedroom. Whenever he played with them he had been careful not to leave them out for his mother to find. He told Margaret not to tell Mother he had them. He wasn't sure why, but he knew she would be mad if she found out Aunt Vera had given them to him. He always knew enough to keep whatever Vera did for them a secret.

Henry sat down on the bed and took a car out. He looked closely at the details on the small red Model T Ford, running the tiny metal wheels along the inside of his hand. Tears streamed down his cheeks. He had treasured these tiny vehicles. "You look after those, Henry," Uncle Jud said the day they let him take them home. "We'll get them back from you when we have a little boy of our own." He had only been five years old, but he sensed a deep sadness on his aunt's face. He had felt like his aunt and uncle had entrusted him with something extremely important, making him even more determined to keep the cars hidden from his mother.

Henry had forgotten all about this box of cars. When Uncle Jud and Aunt Vera finally had a boy of their own, he was grown up and gone. And the little boy had only been three weeks old when his parents died. He hadn't even thought about these cars until he pulled the tin box out just now.

Henry closed the lid and put it in the cardboard box with the few items he was keeping. He set the box on the top shelf in the empty closet.

*

The day ten author copies of *When the Hill Came Down* arrived in the mail, Summer's water broke. When Don entered the house carrying the cardboard box of books he found Summer and Keefe caught up in the frenzy of getting ready to head into Saint John's Regional Hospital. The box sat unopened on the Barkleys' kitchen table in the excitement.

"Your parents, the kids, and Henry and Heather are moving everything into the house today," Keefe told Summer later as they were getting settled on the maternity floor.

"That's a lot of work for them," Summer said.

"I'm pretty sure they don't mind at all. You have your own work to do right here, so don't worry about them. They'll get the bedrooms set up and the kitchen stuff unpacked. You can do the decorating and rearranging when you get back on your feet. Your books came just before we left, you know. Now let's get this baby born, Mrs. Williams."

Two hours later Keefe and Summer welcomed their nine-pound baby boy to the world and named him Judson Donald Williams.

After two days in the hospital Summer was anxious to get home. Don and Marilyn brought the children in to see their little brother and they were excited to get them home too. Heather and Henry were waiting to help Summer get settled before heading back to Ontario.

"I have everything unpacked and got the furniture in place," Heather said. "I didn't want you to have to do it all when you got home, but feel free to get me to change anything if it's not where you want it. It is a beautiful home. Your view of the river makes me wonder if we might just have to move down when Henry retires."

"That would be wonderful. I am going to miss you two, and I know Keefe is sure going to miss you, Henry. The two of you have become like brothers."

*

Keefe drove up to the front door of the Regional hospital

and the nurse wheeled Summer and the baby out on to the sidewalk.

"I think it is silly they make you leave the hospital as if you're an invalid. I had more trouble walking in than I would have walking out now when I can pass this big guy to someone else," Summer grumbled.

"Protocol," Keefe said, opening the car door. "They don't want any lawsuits. Let's get this little guy in his car seat and fastened in and get out of here. Everyone is waiting to welcome you two to your new home."

Keefe drove slowly down the driveway, building the drama of the moment. Pulling up to the house they could see everyone standing out on the front veranda, waving like crazy. Tears ran down Keefe's cheeks.

"I thought I got all the tears out when Paul and Tony were building the verandas and Winston fastened the gingerbread trim on. While Henry and I painted the trim and I bawled almost the entire time. Good thing he's a crier too. Now here I go again."

"You go right ahead and cry," Summer said, her own voice wavering with emotion. "This is huge. You are bringing your own son home to the very place your parents brought you. The house is in a different spot and a lot of years have gone by, but the enormity of it would cause the hardest of the hardhearted to cry. And you, my darling, are not hardhearted. There is not a person here today who does not completely understand what this means to you. Our precious son, the namesake of your father, is coming home. You will give him the life in this place your parents never got the chance to give you. Now park this car and let's get to our homecoming."

"Are you going to carry Mommy over the fresh hold?"

"It's called the threshold, sweetie," Summer said. "Poor Dad will break his back if he tries to carry me."

"I'll take my chances." Keefe laughed as he swept Summer up in his arms. "Welcome to our new home, Mrs. Williams."

Summer looked around at the front entryway. "Behold a Pale Horse" was hanging on one wall, a colourful mat covered the floor, and a large hall tree stood beside the window. "You brought the hall tree from your father's house," she said, turning toward Henry.

"He told us to bring it here," Heather said. "He said it was Vera's and it belonged in your new house."

"Dad told me my grandmother had given it to Aunt Vera," said Henry. "It was the only thing they got out of the house afterwards. The mirror had been shattered and one of the arms on the bench had broken off. He had the mirror replaced and the arm rebuilt. I remember it from my grandparents' house and I also remember the uproar Mom caused when they gave it to Aunt Vera. I was just a kid when I helped Uncle Jud carry it into their front hall. It was always covered with coats at my grandparents', but Aunt Vera refinished it and always kept the wood polished and the mirror gleaming."

"Doesn't a broken mirror cause seven years of bad luck?" Zac interrupted.

"So they say, Zac," Henry answered. "If that's the case, the bad luck when it broke is long over. I was careful bringing it in, though. Wouldn't want any bad luck in this house. There is something else I brought from Dad's house, Keefe, but I'll let you get the little guy settled before I show you."

Summer lifted Judson out of his seat and sat down on the couch with him. "This little guy needs to be fed. Hope you two are all right with seeing me breastfeeding, because I don't plan on hiding away to feed my son. Just give me a minute or two to get situated."

"Zac, let's go get the tin box I showed you earlier," Henry instructed. "It's on the kitchen table."

On returning to the living room, Henry said, "Zac, give the box to your dad. I was supposed to give it to him a long time ago."

"Judson's name is on the cover inside, Dad," Zac called out excitedly. "They're little cars and trucks."

"It is actually your grandfather's name on the cover, Zac," Henry explained. "These little vehicles were his. Tin Toys, they were called, and they were made in the 1920s. When I was a little boy your grandmother used to let me play with them. She gave them to me to take home one day."

Henry turned to Keefe, who was removing the small toys from the box and setting them out on the coffee table one by one.

"Uncle Jud said I was to keep them until they had a boy of their own. I'm sorry I didn't get them to you sooner, Keefe.

I'm sorry I wasn't around all those years. If I'd stayed around or come back after your parents died I could have seen you grow up. I could have seen you play with the toys I loved so much. We could have played with these together. I forgot all about them until I came upon them the other day. As soon as I found the box I remembered what Uncle Jud said the day they let me take them home. I'm so sorry."

Keefe got up and walked across the room to show Summer his father's name etched on the inside lid. "You brought them back at the perfect time, Henry. As soon as he gets big enough we'll all play with them. You're not too old to play cars are you, Zac?"

"No, not if you and Henry are going to play."

"I can play with them too," Melanie interjected. "Girls can play with cars."

"Of course they can, Mel," Marilyn Barkley said. "Your dad said we can all play with them. Grammies can play with cars too. Now, why don't we leave your mom to finish feeding Judson and you can help me set the table for our first meal together in your new house. I made your mother's brown bread rolls, Keefe."

The sun was just beginning to set when Summer and Keefe settled themselves on the front veranda looking out at the calm river. Judson was nestled in his father's arms sound asleep. Keefe wrapped the blue blanket swaddling the infant a bit tighter before speaking. "This has been quite the day, bringing this little guy home, having our first meal in our new home surrounded by family and now sitting out here together in this beautiful place. Tonight, we will sleep under this roof with our three kids and tomorrow we start our life here in this sacred place. I'm overwhelmed with the emotion of it, but mixed up in all of it I keep thinking about Helen and Tom."

"Keefe, you're not going to let them ruin this special day for you, are you?"

"I keep thinking about the lives they lived. They wasted so much, squandered the gifts they were given, and were unable to find any happiness. My parents were robbed of the many years they could have had, but Helen and Tom lost so much as well."

"They had choices, Keefe, and they had responsibility for the choices they made. All their actions had consequences."

"Of course they did, but not everyone has the courage to make the right choices. And not everyone has the ability to understand what really matters. I believe my parents had that. They had courage and clarity. They were kind and generous and appreciated the life they were given. Just like your parents do. Your parents have taught me so much. They get it. They understand what happiness is. They didn't let losing Hudson harden their hearts. They let the things that matter determine their choices."

"Mom says the only control we have in any of it is choosing to be grateful and accept joy."

"Why do you think Helen and Tom could never do that?"

"I think Helen was mentally ill and because of her illness

she let fear, jealousy, and guilt take control. And Tom didn't know how to help her and got bogged down in the misery. It's complicated."

"Complicated, but so damn simple. I think the real work in life is not the building, the farming, the lumbering, the writing, the painting, the making money or raising kids. The real daily labour that needs to be done is working hard to keep a clear vision of what it is in this life that truly matters. This little boy will grow up right here surrounded by love because you and your parents taught me that."

"I think you taught us just as much as we taught you, Keefe Williams."

"Well, whoever taught who, let's make sure we don't forget the things that matter, Mrs. Williams."

"Sounds like a plan, but right now I'm going to take that little boy up to his bed so I can get a few hours' sleep before he wakes me up."

Summer rose from her seat and took the sleeping infant from her husband's arms. "This little guy is some lucky to have you for a dad. What made you so smart, anyway?"

"Well, I did take quite a jar to the head."

Keefe stepped off the veranda and walked a short distance before turning to look up at the gingerbread trim. Tears filled his eyes. Wiping the falling tears, he directed his gaze toward the vast sky above the roofline. He stared at the stunning plethora of colour containing the mixed hues of red, orange, yellow, and purple contrasted by the rippling white clouds and darkening sky. This was the sunset he'd dreamed of painting that evening so long ago when his pencil drew only grey lines on his small scrap of paper.

Acknowledgements

Thank you to Terrilee Bulger and Acorn Press. Thanks again to Penelope Jackson for her editing wisdom and generosity. Thanks to Matt Reid for another great cover.

My dear friend Gladys left us in October leaving behind a rich legacy of story and memory. I was blessed with each moment I spent in her story telling presence. She is reflected in this book through the character of the same name who has many of the same qualities Gladys possessed. When discussing this character and my work on this book with Gladys she remarked 'That's your method', meaning there was a method to my madness of visiting her every week and picking her brain. A method perhaps, but far from madness were the bountiful blessings I received by taking the time to visit and listen to the stories of this remarkable woman. I miss her and will always treasure each story and each memory she shared so willingly with me.

My dad left us in October as well and this will be the last book I will be able to share with him. While staying with me last April he sat in my office for several afternoons while I read the manuscript aloud to him. As I hold this book, those afternoons return to me. I will be thankful for each reader who embraces this book but Dad will remain my most treasured audience and his praise the most valued.

Thanks to Gerard Collins, Janie and all the other writers with whom I experienced Italy. This book blossomed there and grew under the Tuscany sun.

As always thanks to Burton, Meg, Cody, Emma, Paige, Chapin, Brianne, Anthony, Skyler, Bella and Caleb.